The Coming of
the Lords of Chaos

Out of the abyss of time they rode—the powers of darkness, winter, age and death. Stone-grey were their cloaks and boots; their helms and their harness-studs had a dark oily sheen, like slate. Grey, too, were their horses, the pale luminous grey of mist . . .

Their faces dark with anger, they snapped down their visors, lifted their great swords, and plunged straight into the ranks of Faerie. Bushes were trampled, watchfires scattered in the fury of the combat; birds flew up shrieking out of the midnight wood . . .

Siod'h felt Ryll's hand resting gently on his shoulder.

"You see," she said, "that war must go on to world's end, since death has no power to finish it. Friend, do you see now what forces you have chosen to meddle with?"

> "*Songs from the Drowned Lands* has the strength and purity of the old Irish tales fleshed out with a modern storyteller's eye to characterization. I could not stop reading."
>
> —Jane Yolen

SONGS FROM THE DROWNED LANDS

EILEEN KERNAGHAN

ACE FANTASY BOOKS
NEW YORK

For my parents

''Thieras'' was previously published in the Winter 1981 issue of the Van-
couver feminist literary magazine, *Room of One's Own* (a special science
fiction and fantasy issue edited by Susan Wood).

SONGS FROM THE DROWNED LANDS

An Ace Fantasy Book/published by arrangement with
the author

PRINTING HISTORY
Ace edition/June 1983

ISBN: 0-441-77242-0

Ace Fantasy Books are published by Charter Communications, Inc.
200 Madison Avenue, New York, New York 10016.
PRINTED IN THE UNITED STATES OF AMERICA

THE
FIRST SONG

Thieras

Fathoms above her, the darkness paled to a thin green. Frantic, her hands clawing at the black water, she fought her way toward the light. This sea was heavy as stones, unyielding. She tried to cry out, but the sound was trapped in her throat; the black weight of the water lay like a smothering hand upon her face.

She thought, this is death—this is how death feels. And then thought ceased as blindly, desperately, she struggled in the sea's terrible embrace. . . .

Thieras woke, and a great shout at last burst out of her. Hearing that single, agonized cry, the old nurse Muhlwena ran into the room in her nightdress. She caught Thieras in her arms and cradled her like a child.

"Hush, my sweeting. Tell Muhlwena what it is."

"It was a dream," said Thieras, her face buried against

Muhlwena's shoulder. Her heart was pounding in her ribcage like enormous wings. "It was a dream, only. But I will not sleep again tonight. I dreamed of my own death, Muhlwena. I dreamed of drowning."

"Sweet, sweet," the nurse crooned. Her voice was honeyed with love, as comforting as mead. "It was those berries you ate last night—did I not say it was too near bedtime?"

"No," Thieras said. "It was not that." She was calmer now, the worst of the terror fading as the wild rhythm of her heart slowed. "This was not the first time. For months I have had this dream, always the same dream . . . and the same fright after. Only this is the first time I called out so loud, and woke you."

"By the Sea-Mother," said Muhlwena, looking sharply at her. "Such a thing must not be allowed to go on. First thing on the morrow we will send for Fiorag."

"No," said Thieras. There was a stubborn note in her voice now. She knew well enough what Fiorag's cure would be. An overexcitement of the nerves, he would say—and he would prescribe a week in bed. How could she bide indoors in such weather as this?

"It was only a dream," she said. "Go back to bed, Muhlwena. But leave the lamp." And while the old woman hovered uncertainly at her side, she lay back on the pillows, pretending sleep.

She opened her eyes to sunlight. There had been no more dreams. "Muhlwena," she said. "Give me my tunic. I'm going out."

"And not break your fast?"

"I'll dine well enough tonight," said Thieras. "There's a feast, remember." She sat on the edge of the bed to pull her leggings on, and fastened her tunic against the morning's chill.

"It's in rags, that thing." Muhlwena wrinkled her nose. "A king's daughter should not be seen so."

Thieras looked down at the frayed and faded leather. "What, this?" she said fondly. "This belonged to the Falconmaster of the House of Lhuc. There's wear in it yet," she said, "and Longwing knows no other."

She threw the casement wide and leaned out into the morning. It was a day to rejoice in—windless, golden, autumn-tasting. The sky was huge today, vivid as a robin's egg, with only a few ragged scraps of cloud.

She whistled, and from out of that wide blue air Longwing came, dropping quickly to the fist.

"Good morning, my lady." One brown eye looked piercingly round. She was silent and swift as death, this bird: a savage huntress, belonging to herself only, to the wind and the wide sky. And yet she came to Thieras's arm without the lure, on the hint of a whistle, and was content to remain there as long as she was invited.

"We'll go rabbiting," said Thieras. She swung her legs through the window, dropping the few feet to the ground.

Westward, the fields ran swiftly down to the harbor; grey cliffs threaded with pathways, then tier upon tier of rooftops. Across the bay the mists had lifted from the Sorcerers' Isle; the white walls of the temple shone like frost in the clear light. Beyond was the glitter of water, blue as periwinkles, and the sky, enormous, curving down to meet it.

To the east, above her father's house, rose steep slopes of gorse and bracken, through which the grey rocks of these islands thrust like teeth. Higher still there were pine woods—slashed with gullies, bramble-choked, a wilderness. Thieras turned north instead, into open country, moving with her long-legged purposeful stride over the stony meadows, where the goldenrod was just coming into bloom.

She returned to her father's house to find the sun already westering, the sea bright as hammered metal. In the harbor a forest of masts stood black against the dying light. Three fat rabbits hung from her belt—they'd make a stew for tomorrow. Her limbs ached, but it was a good tiredness; the hunt had driven the night-terrors from her head.

She went to the women's quarters to bathe and change. Her cousin Laeli was perched on the edge of the tiled bath, skirt hitched up, one foot resting on a plump knee as she pared her toenails. She eyed with distaste Thieras's wind-tangled hair and dusty tunic, the long smear of rabbit blood across her cheek.

"You're a fine sight for a feast night," said Laeli. "You'd better hurry."

"It's early yet."

"And," said Laeli tartly, "you've a deal to do to make yourself presentable." Her own hair, new-washed and brushed, was ready for plaiting. Her face had a faintly greenish sheen from cucumber-lotion.

Thieras pulled off her tunic and stood waiting for the bath to fill. On the tiled bottom were painted sea-creatures, that seemed to come to life in the swirling water. Gazing at these with studied interest, Thieras said, "Have you seen him yet, our cousin Dhan?"

"Not yet. They say he is more handsome than ever—" Laeli's voice was teasing—"and with an eye for the maids, now that he is a man grown, and a famous warrior."

"He was handsome enough," Thieras said, "but as for the rest, it does not sound like Dhan at all. Do you not remember how shy he was, how serious?"

"Men change, cousin."

Thieras had no answer to that. But after considering her reflection, she sent for the 'tiring-maid Naia to dress her hair. She said to herself, I was a wild girl when Dhan went away to battle. Tonight he will see what a change the years have wrought, in me as well as in him.

Naia's deft fingers had almost finished their task. Now she was fastening baubles to the ends of the long dark plaits— silver apples that moved as Thieras moved, gleaming against the black of her hair, the deep sea-blue of her gown.

Laeli was all in yellow tonight, a vivid daffodil shade that matched her hair. Her slippers were cloth-of-gold, there were gold threads woven into her plaits. That's Dhan's color, Thieras thought, with a pang of jealousy; she remembered how bright his hair had been with the sun upon it. No matter, she told herself, I'll be night to his day; and she smiled, for the fancy pleased her.

In the Great Hall a thousand lamps burned, making a warm yellow cave in that huge-beamed echoing place. The harpers had come, and the first guests were gathering by the fire. The air was full of rich smells and crackling sounds. A whole ox turned on the spit, and the servants, moving among the tables, bore platters of trout and salmon, venison pie, pheasant stuffed with chestnuts. The wine was deep red, unwatered, in silver flagons. Thieras looked with pleasure at the laden trestles; in her excitement, she had eaten nothing all day.

"See," whispered Laeli, pointing. "There he is. There is Dhan." Thieras stood staring, shamelessly, down the length of the hall. This could not be Dhan, surely, this tall, stern, splendid figure, garbed in the sun's color. He was as lean as ever—there had never been much spare flesh about him—but with these years away he had gained breadth and authority. The jaw was more determined than she remembered; the shoulders heavy and the arms great-muscled. She saw that he had a warrior's way of standing, feet firmly planted, quiet and easy seeming, yet never quite off guard.

For three years the tales had come out of the western lands—the sea-raiders driven back, the savage armies routed. There was no harper in these isles who did not sing of Dhan's victories; no maid who had not in secret dreamed of Dhan the Golden. No need to vote, tonight, on the hero's portion. This was Dhan's feast, the celebration of his high deeds, his valor.

They were to sit at one table—Dhan, Thieras, and Laeli.

There was a fourth place laid, for their cousin Siod'h, but he was a serious-minded youth, an acolyte, and would not leave off his studies for feasting.

"Thieras! Is it really you, little cousin?" She felt Dhan's clear gaze upon her. She nodded, suddenly struck dumb with shyness.

"My falcon-maid," he said. Only a manner of speech, but it made the blood rise to her cheeks. "How tall you have grown, and how lovely."

He took both her hands in his, and leaning over the table, he kissed her on the mouth. "In truth, cousin, I am glad to be home."

She smiled, and thought, You have learned more than soldiering, over-water.

With pure malice in her eyes, Laeli said, "She is not always so fine as this. She was hours getting ready. By day she is a hoyden still, and goes about in leggings with her hair unbound."

At that Dhan burst out laughing and gave Laeli a pair of kisses, one on either cheek, which kept her quiet for a while.

They spoke little; only ate, drank the strong wine, and stole curious looks at one another. Then it was time for the harping.

All the songs were of Dhan, in his praise, and he sat quietly, looking down at this plate, perhaps embarrassed a little, as though he wished they would sing of some other hero. Thieras heard those songs with her ears and with her heart.

He was adept in all the arts of war, sang the harpers; a master of battle sorcery. He could draw the sun into an enemy's eyes to blind him, or call up a sudden mist to hide his path. He could trick the eye so that it saw a dozen warriors standing where the mind said there was only one. He had served with that dark warrior Lhuc, whom they called Rock-Sunderer; had stood with him at Moritai, when he called up his ghost-legions out of the hollow hills.

The last harper finished, and returned to his place by the fire. Then they were all calling out to Dhan, bidding him sing; for they remembered that he had no small skill with the harp, and a pleasant voice besides.

So he stood in his yellow cloak with the sun blazoned on it, his tall shadow leaping on the wall; and he sang his own songs, of those battles over-water—blood on the green land, the fallen warriors. He sang in a strong clear voice that had exultation in it, and only a little sadness. War sat lightly on Dhan's spirit, as lightly as his own wounds, healed by herb-magic.

> "Then rose the great axe of Lhuc, rock-splitter,
> then fell like summer grain the men of Mhorav.
> Bitter the cry of the gulls o'er the field of battle.
> Deep and bitter the wounds of the men of Mhorav.
> Bitter and long the lamentations of their widows . . ."

There was to be one singer more, one who sang of love after battle, spring following on winter, the joys of the festive board after long privation; so that the guests might go away from the feast with easy minds, full of pleasant visions. That singer was Eirech of the Silver Eyes, a kinsman of theirs—a distant cousin—whose voice was known in all the Grey Isles, and beyond. He was a graceful, slender young man, with brown cheeks smooth as a girl's, and strange light eyes that slid away from the gaze like silver fish.

As Eirech rose to sing, Thieras saw something harden in Dhan's face. She remembered that there had been no love between these two, as youths.

Dhan said, "He has not changed."

"And I? Have I changed, Dhan?" Laeli, as ever, must turn the conversation to herself.

"Only for the better," said Dhan, but he spoke with his mind elsewhere, as one who humors a child. Thieras noticed for the first time the tracery of fine lines around his mouth and eyes, that gave him a stern look when he forgot to smile.

Then they were all silent, for Eirech had taken up his harp, and the first sweet notes floated through the hall.

His voice was like a shaft of moonlight in the dark forest, a silver chain on velvet. They listened and were enchanted, for his was the purest art of all, the highest sorcery. Thieras felt a joy that was like a hand squeezing her heart, an aching sweetness.

The song was over. Thieras wiped tears from her eyes—furtively, for she did not want Dhan to see. But he was excusing himself, for among the guests there were friends and kinsmen he had not seen these three years.

A soft voice spoke in her ear.

"Do you weep for my song, cousin?"

She looked round and saw Eirech, attentive, smiling.

"It does seem you have the power to make folk sad," she said.

"Oh, never that, hawkmaid. If I thought that I made you sad, I would throw my harp away. It is for beauty, only, that I would make you weep. But listen . . ."

Now he was standing behind Laeli's chair, leaning over her shoulder, his cheek against her hair. "Let us have no talk of sadness. Will you come to my name-day feast, little cousin? And you, hawkmaid?"

Laeli's round pink cheeks grew rosier with excitement. "Your lady mother, will she send for us?"

Eirech laughed. "My mother, what has she to do with it? We are no longer children, cousin." He tweaked her plait. "Or I am not, at any rate. I have my own chambers now, in the Court of the Red Peony. I send my own messages."

"How shall we find you, then?"

"My sweet, you must send your handmaid to ask after me. In the town, they will tell you quick enough where I live."

"And when shall we come?"

"Tomorrow night."

"Thieras, will you come? Think what an adventure—I have never been into the town by myself, without Muhlwena."

"I have," said Thieras. "Many times. But at night, alone?"

"Thieras, come with me." A little girl's voice, wheedling, with an edge of stubbornness to it. "Are you afraid? There is no danger to us, the daughters of sorcerers."

"No danger, perhaps. But what would folk say? Maidens do not go alone into the town at night."

"Thieras, when have you ever given a thought to what folk say?" Laeli seized both Thieras's thin brown hands in her own. She drew her brows together in mock anger, while beneath them her eyes danced. "Dearest cousin, you cannot pretend. You want to go."

Thieras thought of banners flying, the windows of shops, the flower market; lamps glowing yellow in the cobbled streets. And she remembered too what waited in the quiet of her own room—the dark dream, the terror. She sighed, and shrugged. "Maybe it will be all right," she said. "We will take our maids—and it is our kinsman who has asked us . . ."

Eirech kissed his hand to them both, and moved away on his lithe dancer's legs. "Tomorrow," he said, with a last smile over his shoulder.

That night the dream came again, the sea like a mountain moving, the black fear, and she woke in the dark screaming.

"My mind is made up," said Muhlwena, when she had lit all the lamps. "I *will* send for Fiorag."

"Wait a little," said Thieras, pleading. She glimpsed herself in her dressing-mirror. Her eyes looked huge and dark in her white strained face. "Tomorrow I will go to the temple. I will go to Ehlreth, who is Master of Visions. It may be he can look into my mind and drive out these demons."

Muhlwena, who was brewing a tisane at the fire, looked round and said, "Girl, this is not a matter to bother the temple with. There is no sorcery here, surely, only a distemper of the mind, to be cured with a potion.''

Thieras said, ''Ehlreth will not turn me away because it is a small thing and not sorcery. If there is no help for me there—well, then—I will have done with it and you may send for Fiorag.''

The morning that followed was dank and sunless, heavily overcast. Thieras looked out the window, sighed, put on her boots and sheepskin cloak, and set off through the wet fields. A thick autumnal fog had settled over everything—hills, meadow, harbor. It grew colder and more dense as she approached the shore. The tide was in, the sea slate-colored and still as oil. In the dim grey daylight the stones of the causeway shone with damp.

As she walked out onto that broad straight path the mist engulfed her, blanketing her in silence. She could hear only the dull slap of the sea on stone, the cry of the gulls: sounds that seemed to her inexpressibly mournful. Shoreward, the cliffs and the harbor had vanished; ahead loomed the Sorcerers' Isle, a vague mysterious bulk.

She reached it at last, and shivering, stepped from the causeway onto a narrow strip of shingle, plastered with wet weed. Above her, rising into the mist, were walls of deeply fissured granite. A path led upward among tufted sea-grasses and lichened rocks.

At the top of the escarpment she paused to catch her breath. Up here, the mist had thinned to a luminous pearl-grey haze, but looking down she could see the white billowing banks, as thick as wool. Just now a wind had sprung up and was beginning to tear at the edges, ripping them into tattered streamers.

She turned and went on—an easier walk now over the flat bare clifftop. Inland, nearer the temple, gorse gave way to rhododendron and azalea bushes: a wild sea-garden.

Sheltered by pines and sycamores, encircled by tall stones,

the old temple stood as it had for centuries. It had been built in ancient times by the Stone-Masters: a square plain edifice of ice-white marble, made to endure the gales of a thousand winters. Only the long skyward sweep of roof, like a falcon's wing, revealed the sorcery in its design.

Thieras walked up to the great doors of hammered silver; they yielded smoothly to her touch.

Aimlessly at first, she wandered through aisles of white stone columns, slender as flower stalks. Her spirit delighted in this soaring place: the high white walls, the roof curving lightly as a bird's wing on its delicate supports. Lovingly, her fingers traced the pictures on the stone panels, wrought by master carvers in the ancient days. A white world, touched by frost and moonlight, the color of sorcery. Silver pheasants in a silver wood; meadows, dew-silvered, where pale-haired maidens danced. Over the whole an enchantment had been laid, so that walls, ceilings, pillars gleamed faintly with an inner light, as though the moon itself were trapped within.

At length she turned away, remembering her purpose. She said a prayer to the Lady of Mists, the Sea-Mother, and went out again through the little postern door.

Behind the temple, linked by a courtyard, was a long low building of grey stone. Here, in a tangle of dim rooms and branching corridors, the Masters lived: the keepers of charts, the watchers of stars, the pattern-makers.

Thieras went softly along the passages, seeing the flicker of lamps in small spare rooms, the shadows of bent heads. It was always quiet here, a kind of brown hush hanging in the air like smoke, but today it seemed to Thieras there was something deeper than silence. Something that clung like a mist to the faded tapestries, that breathed from the ancient stones: a formless gentle grief, a sad music of the spirit. Perhaps, she thought, it is the season, for there was a bittersweet autumnal quality to it. Whatever the source, it caught at her throat and brought her own melancholy back in a bitter rush.

So, holding back tears, she came to the room where her kinsman Siod'h was learning his sorcerer's arts. He glanced up, hearing her footsteps, and gave her a wan smile.

They were first cousins, she and Siod'h, and much alike, with the same wide sweep of brow under straight black hair, and grey eyes oddly flecked with copper. Often, seeing them together at a distance, folk took them for brother and sister. But Thieras's glance was like the peregrine's, quick and penetrating; Siod'h's eyes, set in the same thin, sculptured face, had a dreaming look about them.

Thieras had not spoken to her cousin for a fortnight, and now she was shocked by the change she saw in him—the deep circles under the eyes, the hollow cheeks.

"You are working too hard," she said, with genuine concern. "You should have come to the feast, Siod'h—we missed you."

He waved a hand at his work-table in wry apology. It was strewn with charts, sketches, sheets of formulae: a clutter to Thieras as awesome and mysterious as the temple itself. Siod'h had chosen the Builder's art, the patient knowledge that shapes towers and temples from raw stone; his sorcery was the Rock-Magic, that patterns the tall stones and binds their ancient power to man's will.

Thieras looked over his shoulder, wondering what manner of task could have brought him to such a state. Spread out in the lamp's circle was a sheet of vellum covered with lines and symbols: a map.

"After all, I think it might be done," he said, as one who continues a previous discussion; though it did not seem that he was talking to Thieras.

"What can be done, cousin?" The intricate marks on the vellum meant nothing to her.

"You see those mountains, there to the north. There are the Blue Stones, the stones of the first and oldest, the most secret power." He broke off, and looked suddenly straight into her eyes, as though just now aware of her presence. "But

Thieras, it will take so long . . ." His eyes were bleak.

"You must leave off for a while," she said helplessly. "You must rest." But he shook his head, and she saw that he was not really listening; his mind was caught up like a netted fish in those lines and symbols.

She wanted to embrace him, to offer him consolation, as she had done when they were children together. But that was a long time ago. Now she was afraid of what she saw in his eyes—a sad knowledge, that she knew would not yield to any simple comfort.

"Goodbye, cousin," she said, with a lump in her throat, and went on, seeking the Dream-Watcher.

"Child, come in," said Ehlreth, seeing her hovering on his threshold. There was welcome in his look, an uncritical affection, and nothing of surprise.

Thieras sat down on a bench, not speaking at first, slowly gathering up her thoughts. In the serenity of Ehlreth's presence, under that mild, grave, penetrating gaze, she felt her mind ease a little.

She glanced around the small, somber room, with no furnishings but a plain oak table, a rough bench, a rush mat on the floor.

"Let me light the lamp," said Ehlreth, for he had been sitting alone in the gloom of the grey afternoon. Huge and vague in the lamplight, their two shapes leaped upon the wall. All at once the words came rushing out: "Dream-Watcher, help me, please, I am so afraid."

Ehlreth pushed back a lock of the silvery hair that had fallen over his brow. His sea-colored eyes were gentle. "You, falcon-maid? What has put fear into that bold heart of yours?"

"Something," she said, "that I cannot bend to my will, that will not obey me as the falcon does. A dream that comes unbidden, and will not let me rest."

"What dream?" he asked quietly.

"I dream of the sea rising up over the dry land. I dream of drowning."

"So," he said. He was not looking at Thieras, but was gazing into the lamp's flame as though he saw something strange and troubling there.

"When you were born I said you would have the gift of vision. I am not often wrong about such things. Look," he said. He was holding something up to the light, a smooth clear stone, a rock-crystal. "I marked you for the one to have this, when I had no more need of visions."

She took it gingerly, between thumb and forefinger, for she was in awe of the old man for all his kindness, afraid of the strong magic at his command.

"Don't be afraid," he said. "There is no harm in it, of itself, only in what you may see there."

She examined it curiously. "What are those marks? I cannot read them."

"No," he said. "You are not ready to read what it says there. One day you might have done. But now . . ." His voice was oddly wistful. "Look into the stone, my daughter. To see clearly takes much skill, but perhaps you may see a little."

She held the stone to the lamplight. She turned it slowly, this way and that, and under her steadfast gaze the shapes took form.

"I see this temple," she said. "And there is Ainn's tower, by the sea, and my father's house."

Suddenly, sharply, she drew in her breath. For behind the dim familiar shapes she had seen something else, a blemish at the stone's heart, a clotted shadow. As she watched, it grew, became a thing that was blacker than night and more terrible: a mountain moving, a vast darkness swallowing up the land.

She thrust the stone away quickly, as though it had burned her. "It is my dream," she said. And she began to weep noisily, brokenly, like a child.

Ehlreth put his hand on her hair—awkwardly, for he was not used to the company of women.

After a moment Thieras lifted her head. In a voice thick with grief she said, "What has brought this ruin upon us? Have we so angered the Sea-Mother?"

Ehlreth said, "It is not her doing. To make the sea rise up like a mountain and devour the land—that power belongs to older and more dreadful gods."

"I do not know these gods," Thieras said.

"No more do any of us. They are the gods without faces and without names, the dwellers in the deep rocks under the sea. They belong to the first days, when there was neither form nor order. They are the Lords of Chaos."

"But we are sorcerers. Have we no power of our own, to bind these gods?"

Ehlreth sighed. "Night after night young Siod'h sits over his charts, scarce sleeping or eating, till I fear for his health. He is seeking a way to bind the sea's power with the patterning of the stones."

"He said to me, 'Thieras, it will take so long.' I did not understand, then, what he meant."

"I am an old man, Thieras. It wearies me to think of such a task as Siod'h proposes. Yet it is the true work of a sorcerer, to restore order to the world."

Thieras's thoughts were eddying, turning, wildly as leaves caught in the wind. "But you have looked into the crystal, Ehlreth. You are Master of Visions. You have seen whether in the end we are saved, or doomed."

"Child, I have seen what may be. That which my blood and my bones tell me will be. But we can reshape the future as the wind shapes the dunes. It is not carved in granite."

"Tell me what you have seen."

"I have seen a circle of blue stones in a high place, a long way off, out of reach of the sea. But it is a broken circle, a pattern never finished. I have seen the sorcerers of these Isles joining their diverse arts—of war, and rune and crop-magic, of weather and healing—into one great pattern turned to a single purpose. Weaving their smaller sorceries together, warp and weft, like skeins of silk, into a strong curtain of magic that must hold back the sea as oiled silk in a window holds back the wind.''

''And then?'' For his voice had trailed away into sadness.

''And then I saw that there were some who had forsaken honor, who had betrayed their art to evil uses. In serving Chaos thus, they had destroyed the order of things, so that the web of magic could not hold. The strands snapped and parted; in that fabric of joined minds a great rent appeared.''

She stared at him, hiding her anguish under a terrible quietude. What could she do, or say? It was there in the stone, the awesome immutable certainty of their fate.

''Child,'' he said gently. ''Thieras. You must go to Ainn. It may be there is no help for any of us now. But what comfort there is left in this world, she will offer you.''

Sick with grief, she found her way out of the temple. As though in mockery the fog had lifted and behind the thin and scattered clouds the sun was shining. It would be hot, later. The sea was a deep azure color, flecked with silver, foaming a little where it washed upon the rocks.

Thieras thought, I will not go to Ainn today. I went to Ehlreth for comfort, and he offered me despair. What more can I ask from Ainn? Tonight she would go down to the town with Laeli, she would go to Eirech's feast. Perhaps there she would find folk who, in their ignorance, could laugh still—who were not afraid to fall asleep.

In the last of the twilight they crept out of doors—not daring to speak until shadowy hills hid the King's House. Breathless and giggling, Laeli ran to keep up with Thieras's long stride as she marched down the sloping meadows.

In deepening dusk they reached the sea-path. The sky was clear now, blue-black, with a scattering of stars. A large pale moon was rising. In the streets of the town the torches were lit; their sharp resiny fragrance mingled with the sea-air and the scent of flowers.

They walked through the marketplace, and Laeli would have lingered awhile, but all at once Thieras could not bear the sight of the silks and the necklaces, the flagons and spice-pots, the rich gaudy array of beautiful objects. As much as music and firelight, the wild hills and the wind, they were part of the life she had loved too well, and had thought must go on forever.

"We'll be late," she said to Laeli, and pulled her along by the hand; till they found themselves wandering among the red columns of the Peony Court.

In a doorway at the street-end a girl with a sweet round face and hard eyes was selling flowers.

"Where is the house of Eirech?" Thieras asked her. She gave them a long look, as though taking their measure, then pointed.

"Take that lane, go up the steps, turn right, and you'll see a second staircase. It's the house at the top, with the dark red door." She sounded as though she had given these directions a hundred times.

They thanked her, and Laeli bought a yellow rose to match her gown.

A staircase of green marble brought them to a tall white house, a crimson door with curious carvings on it.

Standing there on the threshold, Thieras felt a faint prickling at the back of her neck, in the roots of her hair; her stomach tightened.

"Come *on*," hissed Laeli, near-frantic with impatience. Thieras sighed, and raised the silver knocker.

Eirech came to them smiling, his arms outstretched as though to embrace them both. He was as lean and graceful as a deer-hound in his black tunic, his cloak that was silvery-grey to match his eyes. Thieras saw that he was a shade unsteady on his feet; two bright spots burned on his brown cheeks.

"My pretty ones," he said, caressing them with his eyes.

"How delightful to see you. I feared you might not come. You must sit here, one on either hand. So." Wine appeared in silver flagons; dishes of sweetmeats were set before them.

Laeli purred like a cream-fed kitten and sipped her wine; her eyes, gazing out over the silver rim, were wide and glistening.

Thieras glanced round, saw lamplight gleaming in a room full of polished surfaces: mirrors, metals, rich woods. The hangings were red silk, the floors rose-marble, the carpets poppy-colored. Cushions and white furs lay strewn about as thick as clouds.

There was music: a softly strummed lute; drums, muffled and faint as heartbeats. And a great deal of laughter—the voices loud and a little shrill.

Many of the young men were known to Thieras, were hearth-friends of her brothers. But the women seemed creatures of another world. She thought they must stay always in the perfumed courtyards; those white transparent skins were meant to be seen by moonlight only, had never been touched by sun or wind.

Thieras had drunk her wine too quickly, out of nervousness; now, though she thought she had a strong head, she began to feel giddy, her tongue thick and hard to manage. Out of the corner of her eye she could see Laeli's flushed cheeks, the wide flash of her teeth as she laughed, too loudly. But Laeli would have to get by as best she might; Thieras had trouble enough to keep her own composure.

"You are pale, Thieras." Eirech's mouth was close to her ear. "Have you not slept well of late, cousin?"

"Well enough," she said, thinking how rude she must seem, and not caring.

One of his eyebrows lifted, as if to say, "I know better, my girl."

Laeli looked round suddenly, though Thieras could have sworn she had not been listening. "Cousin," she said, "tell him of your dream."

Thieras gave Laeli a look that should have melted the golden apples at the ends of her plaits. But Laeli only returned the stare with bland, unblinking innocence. And Thieras realized that the girl was drunk past any thought of discretion.

"She has this dream," Laeli was explaining to Eirech, who listened with a sudden and terrifying intentness.

"Of what do you dream, little cousin?" asked Eirech, looking strangely at Thieras. "Do you dream of me?"

"She dreams of the sea rising up in its bed, and drowning her," said Laeli. "Every night she wakes up screaming."

Eirech's eyes had narrowed to silver slits. He lifted his flagon, drained it. "It seems you have the gift," he said to Thieras.

"What gift? They are nightmares, only. From growing too fast, Muhlwena says."

"She speaks nonsense, to hide the truth. You have the true sorcery. You can do more than whistle down birds, Thieras. The gods have given you the art of foresight."

"How can you know that? What makes you think I see truly, in these dreams?"

The corner of his mouth twitched, the ghost of a smile. "Because you are not the only one. Do you know Fianna?"

Hearing her name, a lean dark girl turned and raised her hand to them in greeting.

"She has the true gift, Thieras, beyond any doubting. She has told us her dreams."

"And knowing this—you feast and sing?"

"There is not much time left for feasting, or singing either. In the nights that remain there is much I would do, that I have not done."

"And these folk"—she looked round the table—"do they know?"

"They know. Or they guess."

She heard Laeli gasp suddenly with surprise—a shocked, delighted sound. "Look there," the girl said. She made a sweeping gesture with her cup, splashing wine in a red arc across the table.

A woman had climbed up onto the table, had pulled off her flowered headdress and her gown. Now she stood naked in the midst of the company, slender and pale and lazy-eyed, and her smile seemed to mock them. She leaned forward from the waist, and took the flagon out of Eirech's hand. While he watched, while they all watched in silence, she straightened and upturned the cup, letting the dark red wine stream over her breasts, her belly, her flanks. A small ripple of applause went round the table.

The woman stood looking at them with her sleepy eyes. She was grey-eyed, black-haired, one of the old blood, the sorcerers' kind; though in her it seemed the ancient power was spoiled, corrupted. She shook her long hair so that it stood out in a cloud around her head. She turned toward the piper; a curious look passed between them, a wry half-smile, like a secret shared.

The pipes began a new song, languorous at first, then rising, quickening: a high, sweet, spiraling music.

The woman danced, her loins beckoning, but no man among the company moved to join her. They sat as though transfixed, with something that was more than fascination. The music went on. It drove all thought from one's head, so insistent was its rhythm, so intense and piercing was its sweetness.

The lamps burned low; shadows crept into the middle of the room. And then, as the woman danced—as Thieras watched, appalled—those wavering shadows seemed to run together, pooling and thickening like blood. Out of that formlessness a shape appeared, a figure molded like a clay doll out of darkness. It was faceless, this shadow-creature, the limbs without bones, unarticulated; the grotesque semblance of a man. But of its sex there was no doubt; it was singular, crude, oppressive in its maleness.

Thieras stole a glance at Laeli and was repelled by what she saw: the wide rapt eyes, the slackening mouth. This, thought Thieras, this is something that goes deeper than wickedness. To have such powers, and abuse them so . . . It was as Ehlreth had said. For this they had used the arts entrusted to them. For this they had served the gods of Chaos.

The music rose to a pitch that was high and sweet beyond bearing, and ended, the last note hanging in the air like a cry of pain.

It was quiet as death now. All around the table, the banqueters stirred and looked at one another, like sleepers waking in a strange place. Two by two they rose and passed through a curtained doorway, to some inner room.

"Thieras, sweet cousin." A voice in her ear, velvety, insinuating. She turned her head and looked into Eirech's eyes. His breath on her face was hot and pungent with wine.

"Cousin, will you come with me?" He gestured silently with his eyes. Now she saw that the room was empty, inhabited by shadows only. From beyond the curtained doorway there came a soft sound, a woman's laughter.

She shook her head.

"But, cousin, one of you must partner me. There is no one left, and after all, it is my name-day. The feast is in my honor."

"Not I, Eirech. You are not much to my taste, in this mood. You must find someone else." She drained her flagon. "It is late, we must go. They will worry when they find us gone from our beds. Laeli," she said, "call the maids."

"Your maids are asleep," said Eirech. "They have drunk more wine tonight than they are used to."

"Then we must go without them."

"Think for a moment, Thieras. It is not safe for two maidens, walking alone at night in this town."

"Safe as here," Thieras said sharply. "We shall neither of us be maidens long, if we bide here the night."

"Well, hawkmaid, I am too drunk to argue with you. Laeli?"

The girl looked up. She had been cradling her head in her arms, this hour past, but Eirech's voice roused her.

"Laeli, will you come with me, little cousin?"

She nodded and stood up, swaying a little. Eirech put an arm round her waist to steady her, and she dropped her head to his shoulder with a look of sleepy contentment.

"Laeli?" Thieras cried out despairingly. She was befuddled by wine, by the strangeness of this night. She could not think properly, could scarcely speak with any sense.

"Go home, Thieras," said Laeli, and she fitted herself more closely into the curve of Eirech's arm.

"You must come with me."

"You are not my nurse," said Laeli crossly. "There is no one left here for you. You had better go home."

It was very late. The streets were quiet, the windows shuttered. All the stars were out now, thick-clustered as meadowsweet. She could have whistled Longwing out of the night, but there seemed no danger here, in these sleeping lanes. And so she drew her cloak around her, and set out on the long road home.

Silence filled the halls of her father's house. The lamps were out, the fires had burned down to embers. In her own room she found Muhlwena, asleep on a bench by the cold hearth. Lying there, the old woman looked oddly childlike, piteous—a bundle of fragile bones. Guilt stricken, Thieras wrapped a rabbitskin around her, put a pillow under her head. Then she pulled off her own gown and crawled into bed. She left the lamp burning, for she was afraid of the shadows that waited beyond the small circle of its flame.

Thoughts crowded into her head and would not let her sleep. When toward morning she dozed, after a fashion, those thoughts followed her into her dreams:

"You are Thieras, hawkmaiden, daughter of kings. Here you should have ruled in your own time. The shadow of doom that lies over these lands is your doom. The shame that Eirech had brought upon us is your shame also. He is the lord of disorder, the pattern-breaker. He has torn the web that might have held the ocean back. Thieras, daughter of sorcerers, how will you undo what Eirech has done?"

"Thieras!" She sat up. Sunlight was slanting down upon her pillow, and outside the window, a voice called her name. Still heavy with sleep, she drew the hangings aside and looked out.

"On a day like this, how is it I find you indoors, cousin?"

Dhan was wearing an old tunic, faded and much-mended, and high soft boots. There was a wineskin slung on one side of his belt, a satchel on the other. From his gloved wrist a merlin frowned at her with fierce dark eyes.

"Give me an hour," she pleaded. "I'm scarce awake." And she drew her dressing-robe closer under his steady grey gaze.

"You have till I count to twelvescore," he said. She grinned in spite of herself and held up her hand, for he had already begun to count, slapping his hand rhythmically against his thigh. She pulled the curtains shut for modesty's sake and reached for her clothes.

"So, cousin," she said, arriving breathless beside him, her unbound hair caught back with a thong. She whistled for Longwing, who came at once in a rush of wings, as though she too had been waiting. "Where shall we go?"

Always, when she was with Dhan, she was astonished at her own complaisance, her pleasure in following without question.

"Up there," he told her, waving an arm at the wild hills to the northeast. "I remember there is good hawking yonder, and a fine view of the sea."

As she followed him up the steep, heather-covered slopes her spirits lifted a little. The morning was crisp and brilliantly clear, promising heat later. She was at once comforted and excited by Dhan's presence—the aura of strength about him, his easy camaraderie. She watched him covertly, admiring the swift grace of his movements.

"Stop awhile," he said, and she was glad to do so, for the path had grown steep and uneven and she was out of breath.

They were standing on a patch of heathland, banked by tangled shrubbery—hawthorn, brambles, honeysuckle. In the middle of the clearing were two huge boulders, blue-grey and yellow with lichen. Thieras scrambled to the top of the taller one; from this vantage point she could look down over the whole western side of the island, lying shadowless in the noonday sun.

She gazed with a sad affection at the summer landscape: the soft purple-grey of the heather, like smoke, the red and gold of the gorse on the stony hillsides. A long way down she could see the pale curve of sand dunes; dark-green bands of seaweed on a grey beach; and then a silvery dazzle that hurt the eyes.

"What do you see?" Dhan asked. He was standing with his face upturned to her, squinting against the sun.

"All that I love in this world, and must lose," she wanted to tell him. But she said nothing, only smiled, and beckoned him up beside her.

They sat there for a while, drinking wine, sharing the bread and cold fowl from Dhan's satchel. The hawks, waiting, circled in the bright air.

Then they went on up the slopes, through the rusty bracken, picking their way over broken stone. Toward mid-afternoon they came out on a bare hilltop that overlooked the sea. Nearby, among gaunt lichened trees, was a chamber-tomb. It had been sealed up for centuries, was matted over with brambles and long grass.

At the sight of that humped shape, the anguish of the night rushed back upon Thieras, sudden as a blow to the chest, oppressive and crippling. She turned away, staring seaward, hoping Dhan would think it was the salt-wind that brought tears to her eyes.

"Thieras?" A hand on her shoulder, forcing her gently round, grey eyes narrowed, searching her face. "Thieras, what troubles you?"

"The tomb," she said, trying to swallow the great lump in her throat. "I cannot bear to look at it, it makes me think of dying."

She told him that; it needed less explaining. But had she been honest, she might have said, "It is not the presence of death that makes me weep. I grieve for the loss of my own tomb-place, my birthright; the place I was promised among the bones of kings. Now it seems I must meet death alone, without kin, without friends; and the terrible sea will scatter my bones."

"Listen to me, cousin," Dhan said. His eyes were somber now, and deep enough to drown in. "I know there is more wrong than you will say. Your face—and the Mother knows I love it better than any on earth—your face has grown white and thin, and your eyes are as big as the night owl's. I would give much to hear you laugh, Thieras."

She stared at him. He seemed a creature made of sunlight, with his yellow hair, his eyes that in this bright weather were more blue than grey. There were no shadows in his heart. How could she tell him of that dark knowledge that possessed her?

"Thieras," he said again, very softly, and his hand cupped her chin. His mouth was close to hers. In spite of everything, she observed that it was a wondrously well-shaped mouth. "Little cousin, I am going away soon, I am sailing south to the old lands—to Aprilioth."

"So far?" she managed to say. "And when shall I see you again?"

"Thieras, you know you will not see me again. Not if you stay in this doomed place."

So there it was, falling like a shadow between them, the

thing that was unspoken, and unspeakable. She was the first to break the long silence, asking, "You also, Dhan? Have you the gift of sight?"

He shook his head. "I have not your gift—or your curse. But I have been to see the Dream-Master."

She looked at the ground and in a hoarse whisper said, "You are a warrior. A warrior does not run away."

"But he must retreat sometimes. It's his business to know when the odds are impossible—and to save what he can."

She made no answer. She was weeping openly now, bitter tears that would not be checked.

"Thieras," he said, "I will not leave you here. There is a place on my ship for you . . ."

Stubbornly, fiercely, she shook her head.

"Why do you say no? Are you afraid of the voyage?"

She almost smiled at that, through her tears. She thought of the south—the jeweled sea, the burning light, the white towers of Aprilioth. By Dhan's side, in those luminous seas, what dangers could she not face? Storm, siege, all the monsters of the deep—they would be nothing to her. And yet it was true, she was afraid. She had lain with fear for a long time; it was a cold and comfortless lover.

Suddenly she hid her face in the hollow of his neck, feeling the hard shape of the bones under the skin, hearing his breath quicken against her hair. His arms tightened around her.

When she looked up her voice was even again, her face composed. "I cannot go with you, cousin."

"You must."

"No." Her throat hurt, she was weary of talking. "Don't ask me for reasons. I only know that I will stay. That I am meant to stay."

She must not let him know how her heart, her blood, cried out, "I will go." But while she could, she would touch a little of that fierce light burning in him, hoping it might warm her in the grey times.

"Cousin," she said, and it was barely a whisper. "Anyway, will you stay with me for a while?'' She drew him into the gloom of the tall bracken, and there they made for themselves a cave, a hidden place.

Ainn's tower was a slender grey shape rising out of the grey rock. So near was it to the shore that at high tide the sea lapped at the foot of her staircase, and all winter the gales battered at her casements.

Everywhere on these rocks the sea-birds nested—terns, petrels, grebes, curlews, puffins. When Ainn walked on the shore they would come to her without fear, circling and crowding close to her; through their shrill, shifting ranks she moved like a queen among courtiers.

There were butterflies too, in this soft weather—a garden of yellow and silver wings at Ainn's windows.

Thieras climbed up the narrow sea-worn stairs. The door to Ainn's dayroom stood open; she knocked softly and went in. This was a homely, pleasant room, with no more furnishings than one woman needed: a few chairs, a dresser for the plates, a table. The only luxury here was a carpet woven in deep southern colors—an intricate pattern of birds and blossoms.

Ainn was standing at the window, watering the herbs that grew everywhere in pots and baskets. Their sharp subtle fragrance filled the room. She smiled, and held out her two hands to Thieras. The old blood, the sorcerers' blood, ran true in Ainn, as it did in Thieras—showing in the brown, slender face, with bones that were a shade too strong for beauty, in the clear wideset grey eyes.

Today there were deep shadows under those eyes. Ainn's face had a drawn, tired look, as though she had gone too long without sleep.

She knows why I have come, Thieras thought, as indeed Ainn knew most things, without needing to ask.

''You are weary,'' Ainn said, ''and unhappy.'' She seemed to take no account of the tiredness in her own eyes. Her voice offered rest, solace—unstinted, unquestioning.

"Sit here by the window. See, I have made spice cakes, and there is wine from last year's blackberries."

Thieras saw that the table was laid, with beakers and the good plates of painted ware. "You knew I would come today."

"Perhaps." A sweet, slow smile, as she set down the cakes, still hot from the oven. In that smile there was uncomplicated pleasure at Thieras's visit; though behind, in the eyes, pain lingered.

The smell of the cakes was intoxicating. Thieras, who was suddenly famished, ate four of them while Ainn banked the fire and pulled her stool to the table.

"So," said Ainn, pouring wine. Her tone was matter-of-fact. "One should eat before facing a difficulty. And drink a little wine. It makes thinking easier."

She looked suddenly into Thieras's eyes, and Thieras caught her breath at what she saw there.

"It will come, child," Ainn said. "In all these isles there is not power enough to stop it. Too many have lost faith, have forsaken the hard path. Sorcery lends itself to other uses, besides the true one."

Thieras felt her throat tighten. "Eirech—in his house, last night . . ."

"Yes. And what you saw there was the beginning."

Thieras's mouth was dry. She lifted her cup, her hand trembling a little, and swallowed it at a draught, like one of Fiorag's potions.

She stared down at the empty beaker.

"Once," she said, "when I was little, I dreamed that my grandfather was dead. And when they told me that he had died in truth, I was sore afraid, and sorry, for I thought that I had made him die by dreaming it."

"Child," said Ainn gently, "you have the sight. You saw what was to come. You did not make it happen."

"But it seemed to me then—" Her voice shook, so painful was the memory of that long-hidden guilt.

"Look out there," said Ainn, and she pointed to the window. "Do you see that flock of gulls, yonder? Do you see the waves breaking on the rocks?"

Thieras nodded.

"You see them. Yes. But did you have any hand in bringing them here?"

Thieras gave Ainn a wan smile, and let it seem that she was comforted. But still the old guilt lingered, a thing beyond argument, outside of logic.

For a while there was silence between them. Ainn sat waiting for Thieras to speak, her brows drawn together in gentle inquiry.

At last Thieras looked up and said, "You know that Dhan is going away. He is going to the old lands."

"And you, Thieras?"

"I will stay."

Ainn said, "Child, have you counted the cost? With death so near, the heart cries out in loneliness. The flesh hungers. It is a hard time to be alone."

"You are alone."

"My Lady is jealous. Who cleaves to her, cleaves to no other."

Thieras cried out suddenly, "Ainn, tell me the spell. Tell me what I must do, that She will come to me."

"I will show you where you may find her. But you must go to her with a quiet mind." She touched her cool fingers to Thieras's temples. "I can feel your blood pounding there, like a drum beating. There is a storm in your eyes. Look at me, Thieras."

Ainn's eyes were wide and calm, grey as the light that comes before the sunrise. She grasped Thieras's two hands, which had been fluttering in her lap like birds. "Be still, my daughter. Be still awhile. And look at me."

She held Thieras's hands so tight it seemed their pulses beat as one. And drawing that sad restless spirit to her, Ainn worked her gentle sorcery.

This was a magic stranger than any other, this meeting and intermingling of two souls; one spirit flowing imperceptibly into another, as a stream flows into the sea. A great calm descended upon Thieras in that tranquil luminous place. The light of Ainn's soul was the radiance of the sea at dawn, rose-pink and golden; a green space in a summer forest. She sheltered there, as a bird shelters from the storm: at peace with herself, at one with Ainn.

"Go to Her now," Ainn said. "She is waiting." And Thieras went down from Ainn's tower into the world of men, where mists gathered as the light faded, and the sea on the rocks was grey as flint.

They walked together along the darkening shoreline, coming at last to the sea-caves. "There," said Ainn. "There is time enough, before the tide turns. Go now, Thieras."

The black entranceway swallowed her up. She could not see anything at first—had only the sense of great space, vaulted, echoing. She went on slowly, feeling her way along the wet weedy floor. A chill mist had seeped in after her, rising off the sea.

Briefly the sun must have slipped from behind the clouds, for a shaft of light pierced the deep gloom of the cave's belly. In that huge arched space it cast only a faint glow, a yellow shimmering. Then abruptly it faded as the sun set.

Thieras stood there for a long time, in a silence so profound that she could hear the sighing of her own breath, her heart beating. "Lady," she whispered at last. "Lady, do not abandon me here."

She waited. And as she stood in that gathering dark that seemed in itself a kind of death, she thought: The end will be quick when it comes, maybe I will be asleep. I could ask Fiorag for poppy-juice, and it would be a last sleep, without dreams, and with no waking.

"Thieras." It was there, as though a veil had lifted: a presence, a whisper in the mind, not heard but felt. A momentary brightness, like the sun on water; a power enduring as the earth itself, sweet as turned soil in spring. It was there, the thing that Thieras sought; though she could neither see it nor reach out to touch it. There was a strange solace in it, a strength beyond herself, that she could lean on; and terror deeper than any she had known.

A voice, that might have been the wind's voice, said: "For you there will be no wine, no poppy. That is not the way a king dies, or the daughter of kings. A king does not run from death, nor does he bargain with it. Thieras, if there is the true blood of warriors in you, you will not let death strike you from behind. You will hold out your life in your two hands, a gift freely offered. That is the order of things—the first and ancient order—and you will not betray it."

Thieras folded her deerskin leggings, her falconing coat, and put them with her boots in the chest. The late afternoon sun through the window showed a furring of dust on the lid. How careless the maids had grown, in these last days. She fetched a cloth, and polished the deep-carved oak.

She straightened the coverlet, plumped the cushions on her bed, and drew the curtains against the sun. Already the room had a bare, sad look about it, like a place where nobody lived.

Muhlwena was nodding, half-asleep in her chair.

"I'm going out for a while," Thieras said softly. Startled, the old woman looked up at her. "Girl, the day's near ended. Promise me you'll not wander far?"

"Not far," said Thieras. "I promise." She bent quickly and kissed Muhlwena's cheek. It felt dry and soft to her lips, like kidskin. She closed the door behind her, gently, and went out through the empty corridors of her father's house.

She loved this stretch of rocky coast, where great billows and drifts of sea-pink softened the ancient stones. The sun lay upon the water, burnishing its placid surface; the light that filled the world was yellow and thick as honey. Soon now, the sun would slip below the horizon, and its light would fall on older stones than these.

A child with a reed-pipe was sitting cross-legged on the breakwater. To Thieras, the thin high sound seemed full of a melancholy sweetness. Tears sprang suddenly to her eyes. I cannot leave this place, she thought. There was a pain in her breast, like a hand tightening round her heart. Her throat was clotted with the tears she had not shed. And then she thought, but we must all leave it, one way or another.

The hawk was a sleek warm weight on her wrist. "Go, Longwing," she whispered. "Find Dhan. The sea will not take you, or him either." And she watched the bird soar up and up, till she vanished at last beyond the cliffs.

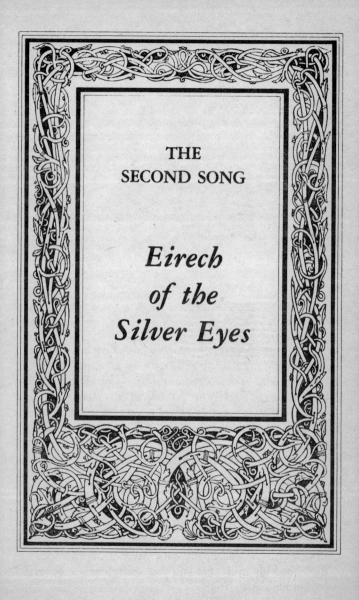

THE
SECOND SONG

*Eirech
of the
Silver Eyes*

Propped gracefully on one elbow, Eirech watched the little servant reaching up to light the deck-lamps. She was a favorite of his—sweet, timorous, scarcely more than a child. In a moment of whimsy he had ordered her dressed in panels of gauze that at every breath of wind revealed her young breasts, her smooth brown flanks. The effect was, as always, charming.

Her task finished, the girl turned, dipped a shy curtsy, disappeared. Eirech yawned, and his pale gaze slid over the barge-side into the waters of the bay. The wind had risen, breaking the mirrored lamplight into fragments, a thousand yellow candles in the blue-black water. They flickered there like the lights of some drowned sea-king's palace. Warm though the wind was, Eirech felt a shiver run down his spine. He closed his eyes—but still that unsettling vision clung behind the lids.

The mood of the soft evening was broken. Restless and irritable, he sat up cross-legged on his heap of cushions.

The Lady Arianth turned to him with a drowsy smile. Her lap was piled with red roses, full-blown in the summer's heat. One by one, with lazy patience, she was tearing off the petals and dropping them into the bay.

Eirech said to her with a kind of vexed surprise, "Can there be any more dreary occupation, than waiting for the world to end?"

"Still and all," said Arianth, "it has not ended yet." She sighed and shook out her gown, scattering rose-petals across the deck; leaning sideways, she nuzzled Eirech's cheek with her soft pale lips.

"Clearly," said the Lady N'hadha, "you should fill your hours in some less tedious way." She was standing at the bow, letting the wind stream through her coppery hair. She arched her slim back, pushing her breasts out, conscious of the picture she made, like a carven ship's goddess.

"Did you know," she said, "that Ahren the artist has undertaken to sculpt me in ivory? He is fashioning an image so small it may be hidden under a rose-leaf, yet so wondrously fine in detail that one might believe it breathed, and lived. It will be his masterpiece, the ultimate expression of his art, mirroring not only my outward self, but my very soul. It will take him a year to finish, he says."

"And where will Ahren the artist be in a year?" asked Arianth scornfully. "At the bottom of the bay, with the rest of us, and his masterpiece too, for the fishes to wonder at."

N'hadha looked at her with obvious dislike. Coolly returning the stare, Arianth continued, "The warrior Dhan is fitting up a ship that will take him south, to the old lands. I asked to go with him—but he says he will take only those who have the arts of wind and weather magic, or those with the strength to use an oar." She pouted. "I vowed I would be of more use to him on board than any wind-sage, but one cannot reason with such a man."

Grey-eyed Dhagha looked up. In her slow, deep, beautiful voice she remarked, ''There is a great deal of water betwixt here and the old lands—and the fine weather near gone. In the end he will be drowned the same as we are.'' She too had begged to go with Dhan, and to her chagrin, had received the same reply.

''Siod'h the Builder,'' said Arianth, ''is fetching stones by land and water from the Holy Mountain. He means to build a Great Circle, one with the power to hold back the sea.''

''Another madman,'' said N'hadha, turning round suddenly, so that her hair whipped across her face. Impatiently she caught it back with both hands. ''In the temple they invent work to keep from thinking. He is a dry sapless stick, that Siod'h. Can he think of no better way to spend his last hours, than on a fool's errand like that?''

''And you, Eirech?'' The sorceress Dhagha was watching him, teasing him with her sly, one-sided smile. He looked down into grey eyes the color of woodsmoke, in which an ancient and unfathomable knowledge dwelt, and then into Arianth's blue, round, deceptively innocent gaze.

''I?'' said Eirech. ''I mean to end my days as I have lived them, in the tireless pursuit of pleasure. It has been my experience that true ecstasy has the power to blot out pain. Else, my sweet—'' and with his small sharp teeth he seized the rosy tip of Arianth's ear—''else I would not have made love to you with such relish as I did last night, on the cold sand, with barnacles scraping my knees.''

''Yet I am weary of this place,'' said N'hadha. ''We have rung all the changes. Every night is the same as every other night. We eat, we drink, we make love to one another—and we sleep. On the sea-roads to Aprilioth, where Dhan is going,'' she said wistfully, ''there are marvelous kingdoms, stranger sights than any in these isles.''

''Or,'' mused Dhagha, falling in with the game, ''there are the wild lands northward, where the sea cannot reach. I have seen the men of those tribes, when they came to trade furs and flint. Wild folk out of the northern woods, in skins, with bones round their necks. Think how it would be to lie with such a one—like lying with a wild beast." As she spoke an odd light flared in her eyes.

Arianth shuddered delicately. "Must you speak of such things? Better to die here, cleanly, when the sea comes, than to be ravished by wild men."

"Possibly she is right," said N'hadha. "Such pleasures are better in the imagining, I would think, than in the event."

"And think of the journey," said Eirech. He fell back on his cushions with a pained look, while Arianth, murmuring endearments, stroked his brow. "Mountains and gullies to climb over, brambles in your hair and stones in your boots. Dried fish and barleycakes, sour beer; the hard cold ground to sleep on. Do not speak of it, my sweet ones. There is enough pleasure to be had in these isles, if we search for it diligently. While we wait, let us make such a game of love as this age of the world has not seen." He sat up suddenly, inspired. "This task I assign to you, my beautiful witches: that on each night for three nights you shall prepare for me an entertainment, a pleasure-feast. You shall discover ways to delight my eyes, my spirit and my flesh. You, sweet Arianth, you shall go first, then you, my impetuous N'hadha. And last of all, you, my sorceress—" This was to Dhagha. Eirech had cause both to fear and to rejoice in her dark powers.

"It sounds a pleasant enough diversion," N'hadha said. "And what prize goes to the victor?"

"A song," said Eirech of the Silver Eyes. "She who delights me most, shall have a song meant for her ears alone—the sweetest song sung in a thousand years, a song to comfort her when the world ends."

"Then I must win," said Arianth. Bold and guileful as a kitten, she gazed at him out of her great sky-colored eyes. "For I believe there is no sweeter voice than yours in all the world."

"Nor," said N'hadha, with only a hint of mockery, "is

there any handsomer face in these isles, feet quicker in the dancing, a form more graceful.''

"And . . ." Dhagha's lips curved in that wry lopsided smile, "if there is one who has better mastered the arts of love, I have not met him yet.''

Eirech smiled, for like an actor he lived much in the eyes of other folk, and praise was the breath of life to him. He looked into those three intent and lovely faces, saw their eyelids grow heavy, their cheeks flush with the quick stirrings of desire. His soul expanded. "Come, witches," he said, and drawing aside the curtains he led them into his cabin, where the lamplight fell on teakwood chests inlaid with jade and porphyry, on tapestried walls and silken sheets.

He stole a sidelong glance in the mirror of polished bronze that stood beside the bed, noting the long eyes the color of frost on stone, the thin fine features, the dancer's limbs. He reached out for a moment as though to embrace his own gleaming image, but he had not magic enough for that, and so he drew the three women into the circle of his arms instead.

Before the next day's light had faded the Lady Arianth was at his door. "Hurry," she said. She was smug and sly with secrets. In a bemused silence he followed, as she led him through the streets of the town, up the cliff path and over the high stony meadows.

Inland, the fields were purple with vetch and foxglove, dusky gold with bracken; the seaward slopes still gilded by the dying light. He had not guessed it could be half so pleasant here, on a summer's eve.

Arianth stopped, turned. The wind had reddened her pale cheeks and tumbled her hair. She was panting with the unaccustomed exercise; a film of moisture shone on her smooth brow, her delicate upper lip. Eirech thought he had never seen her look so disheveled—nor so enticing.

They had come to the edge of a poplar wood, in that lovely hour of evening when the rich light, the color of amber, falls slanting through the leaves. Arianth took his hand and drew him in among the trees, into a green and golden room of sunlit branches, dappled shadows, columns of poplars straight as spears.

"Look," she said, "I have ordered a banquet prepared for you," and he saw that under the trees, on a trestle of rough planks spread with a coarse cloth, a rustic feast, a picnic had been laid.

He watched with wry amusement as Arianth uncovered the dishes: hazelnut meats, wild honey and clover-bread, acorn cakes and watercress, rosehip tea and blackberry wine . . .

"And the other guests? I see two places only."

"You are the only guest, my dear. With me to attend you. We are the only two mortals in this wood."

She bade him be seated, and offered him her wildwood delicacies. He took some of each to humor her, but ate little, only nibbled on a morsel of bread; for though the game amused him, he feared for the effect on his stomach of this odd fare. The wine, though coarse, was pleasing, and he let her refill his tankard as often as she liked.

"So," said Arianth, finally. She stood up, brushing crumbs from her lap, and led him from the table. The rich light was fading now, shadows running together beneath the trees.

"What now?" he whispered.

"Wait," was Arianth's reply. "Only wait. And listen."

And then it seemed to him that there was a hint of movement, laughter, just beyond the limits of his senses. Half-glimpsed among the branches, in the shadows, something watched him: vague shapes, a myriad of curious eyes. He heard the sound of pipes, a delicate high music; it seemed to come from above, from all about him, from the darkening air.

He said, "You swore we were the only two mortals in this wood . . ."

She smiled. "We are."

"And these?"

"The dwellers in the forest. They belong to another world, not ours."

She called out softly, the syllables of an old enchantment. He had heard such spells used to summon down birds, to call the wild deer from out of the wood.

From among those shy elusive forms one shape emerged—the slim figure of a girl. She stepped boldly out of the shadows: a creature long-limbed, sapling slender, with huge eyes of gold-flecked green. Her flesh seemed translucent, as delicate and easily bruised as petals.

She came to Eirech, laughing, with a sly conspirator's glance at Arianth. When she touched his hands with her long thin fingers he could see all the intricate patterning of the bones beneath the skin.

Hovering there, it seemed she might blow away on a breath of wind, and yet her great eyes as she gazed at Eirech were full of a teasing invitation.

He lay with her on the soft moss under the trees, in the green gloom. She seemed to him a creature impossibly fragile, not fashioned from flesh and bone like other women; a being of no more substance than the wind in the branches, the green light netted in the leaves. What happened between them was sweet and strange, and left Eirech with more than the ordinary sadness that follows love. He knew that a longing had been awakened in him, that might find no fulfillment in this world.

N'hadha woke him without warning in the grey hours before dawn, hammering furiously on his chamber door.

"Woman," he groaned, "what madness is this? Come to bed, or be gone."

"I'll do neither," she retorted, as she stripped back his counterpane. "You asked for a pleasure-feast, and I have prepared one. We will dine at sunrise, by the edge of the sea."

And so, cursing all the while that he shook sleep out of his eyes, he dragged on his tunic and boots, threw a cloak over his shoulders and followed her through the chill mists down to the shore.

At this strange hour between darkness and dawn the sea lay quiet, a vast featureless grey plain, lightening only a little where it met the grey horizon. The tide, receding, had left dark bands of seaweed straggling over the pale sands. Wet black rocks crouched at the sea's edge like sleeping beasts.

Eirech shivered, and hunched his shoulders under his cloak.

"Woman," he said plaintively, "where is the pleasure in this? Let me go back to my warm bed."

"Wait," she said. "Have a little patience. The dawn is only a breath away."

He looked up, and saw a faint glow starting in the eastern sky, above the cliffs: a delicate flush of rose and pearl. Moment by moment the sky lightened and color crept back into the world.

All the while, N'hadha had been gathering bits of driftwood; now, crouching on her heels in the sand, she produced tinder and flint from her pouch and made a fire out of the wet wood. She knew many such small useful spells, and took great pride in them.

Soon she had their breakfast spread out on a clean cloth on the sand: oysters gleaming damply in their shells; thin strips of salmon; crab, lobster; white bread with a golden crust. And spiced wine, mulled over the fire. This, thought Eirech, was a cut above Arianth's rough peasant fare, this was food fit for a sensitive palate. For all that he must consume it at such an hour, in this dismal place, at N'hadha's mad whim.

And then, because he was accustomed to breakfasting in bed, his thoughts turned inevitably to other matters.

"So," he said, licking clam juice off his fingers, "so, my girl, shall we return to my rooms? While I am still in a mood to forgive you?"

"Not yet," said N'hadha. "And I ask no forgiveness, either."

She closed her eyes, and there poured from her throat a strange, shrill lament, as harsh and desolate as a gull's cry. It brought to Eirech's mind the shriek of the wind over the gaunt cliffs, the calling of one lost ship to another in the shrouding mist. And yet there was sweetness in it too, as there was sweetness in the dawn's sudden light over the sea.

Then faint and soft, from some far-off place, an answering music came. There was a flash of something silvery, sinuous; long wet hair glistening in the light; a woman's face, arms, shoulders; high round breasts, perfect breasts, touched by the first rays of the sun. Eirech felt a quick rush of astonishment, then a great and marveling curiosity. N'hadha's gift, this—as strange and unforeseen as Arianth's had been.

But afterwards, with the taste of salt on his lips, the smell of the sea clinging to him, despair returned like the inrushing tide.

For an hour or more he sat cross-legged on the white sand, with his chin sunk in his hands, cursing the sea's sun-spangled, treacherous beauty. How would the end come? he asked himself. For come it must, as surely as the tides rose. They knew their work well, those star-watchers, dream-watchers, keepers of charts. They left no space for hope; no corner, however narrow, where a man might hide from the truth.

Would the sea rise slowly, imperceptibly, the tide each night creeping a little higher on the shore? Or would it come raging like a wild beast out of its bed, catching them up like bits of straw and dashing them upon the rocks? The first of these, he thought, would be the more terrible. He shivered to think of how it must feel—to watch the slow, insidious, inescapable approach of one's death. Better that death should catch him unawares, take him with wine in his belly, a woman in his bed.

N'hadha, who had been dozing, stirred and sat up.

"Look," she said. Eirech turned and saw approaching across the sands a tall, slender, grey-robed figure. Shorebirds by the hundreds—terns, kittiwakes, petrels, curlews—billowed and surged about her, or trailed behind in ragged procession. Overhead, the air was dark with wings.

"It's early for you to be abroad, Eirech. And you, N'hadha." A wry, gentle, humorous voice. He looked up into the grey eyes of the sorceress Ainn. The birds seethed about his ankles, a raucous tide of grey and tawny plumage.

"We had a fancy," he lied glibly, "to see the sunrise over the water. There are not a great many dawns left to us, if we are to believe what the priests say."

"Not many," said the Lady of the Birds.

"But in the end," Eirech said, "it was not worth the trouble of rising early. Nature, in her raw state, I find no more enticing than I find a woman when she first wakes—when she is unadorned, uncoiffed, disheveled." He said this with a certain wicked relish. He found her tedious, this priestess with the calm tired face and the searching eyes. He saw too much strength in her features, too little of ordinary prettiness. There were deep lines meeting at the corners of her eyes, a broad streak of grey in the fading chestnut hair. Eirech had no time for plain women, nor aging ones.

And this one, he knew, could see straight into his head, with those eyes the color of the winter sea.

Beside him N'hadha said, "I don't want to die." Her voice was childishly petulant. "You belong to the temple, Lady. Tell us why the priests can do nothing to help us."

Ainn's face clouded. She said softly, too softly, as one who struggles to curb her anger, "Girl, you have done nothing to help yourself. It is Chaos itself that is unleashed upon us. In the temple they are fighting—with the last strength that remains to them—to impose order upon the world. Perhaps they might have succeeded, were it not for those who have courted Chaos, who have perverted the true order of things." Her grey eyes looked coolly into N'hadha's green ones. "One sorcerer alone cannot bind the Old Gods—a hundred, a thousand sorcerers together might manage it. It is a fearsome sight, to see the joined power of our people. Yet one man alone, or one woman, forsaking the true path of magic, has the power to break the web."

N'hadha shifted uncomfortably under that mild relentless gaze.

"There are locks on the doors that divide the world of men from other worlds. One does not tamper with those locks for any trivial reason—out of curiosity, for private pleasure."

"Eirech," said N'hadha, in a voice of wintry sweetness, "it is late and I wish to sleep." Like a sullen child she turned away from Ainn.

Following N'hadha along the sunlit beach, Eirech felt on the back of his neck the weight of Ainn's grey gaze. Was it a reproach, that look, or a warning? Her image seemed burned on his brain—the tall, spare, solitary figure, commanding her lonely stretch of shore as though it were a high king's court, and she its queen.

At midnight Dhagha came to him. Heavy with dreams, he woke disoriented, uncertain of time or place. Dhagha's face swam before him in a room full of leaping shadows.

"Come," she whispered. "It is time for the third feast—the last and richest banquet."

"Where are you taking me?" he wanted to know.

"Not far," she replied, pressing her fingers to his lips. And she led him through the sleeping streets to the door of her own house, three lanes away in the Amethyst Court.

In her bedchamber, banks of scented candles filled the air with a musky fragrance. She pushed aside a curtain, drew him into a room that was like a warm dark cave, furnished with cushions and a single ebony chest.

She held up the lamp; in its dim glow he could see the antique carvings on the chest, the inlaid pattern of vines and blossoms in opals, lapis, cinnabar.

"Here is my feast," she said, "a banquet not only for the gross appetites of the flesh, but for all of the senses."

She threw back the lid of the chest and revealed what lay within: a glittering array of jars, phials, flagons, caskets.

Eirech shivered a little in the warm room. All of his art was in his voice; knowing little of magic, he feared this woman's powerful sorceries.

Dhagha held up a jar of iridescent purple glass. "This comes from Shaa'lan, that city that is half as old as earth itself; where pleasure is the one art, the final wisdom, for which all other pursuits have been abandoned. Bathe in the oil of Shaa'lan and the body opens to delight as a flower to the sun. Through every pore the skin drinks in sensation, with senses so exquisitely sharpened that pleasure rises to the edge of pain."

"And this." She opened a gilded box filled with a sweet-smelling pollen. "A sailor brought me this, all the way from the Vale of Ihriz, in the Land of Amar. That night we burned it like incense beside my bed, and the pleasure we had was prolonged for what seemed an eternity—continuing through all the hours of that night and all the day that followed, only ending at sunrise on the second day."

"Or this." She showed him a phial filled with a fine greyish dust. "It looks like nothing more than common earth. Yet, Eirech, to what realms have I been transported—I have been to countries that are on no map of earth, where jewels hang upon the trees like blossoms, where crystals fall from the air like summer rain." She shook the phial and watched the contents settle, then returned it carefully to its place. "But we must have guests to our banquet. Who would you have me summon? The mountains and seas are no barriers, nor time, nor death, nor any boundaries of the natural world."

"Dhagha, my witch, you know my tastes better than I know them myself. I leave the choice in your hands."

And so she closed her long smoke-colored eyes, and

gathered her powers to her. To the feast she summoned
queens of far lands, ladies of ancient days, each one a rare
jewel prized for her beauty in her own time and her own
place.

The first of these was a pale-skinned northern princess
wrenched rudely from her bed, blue eyes wide with astonishment, yellow hair falling over white shoulders like the
sun on snow. She was a maiden, afraid and unwilling, till
Dhagha gave her wine that roused in her an uneasy passion.

After her came a languid desert woman, and then a fragile
exquisite lady in patterned silks, from the court of an eastern
king.

Dhagha's eyes shone with a feverish glitter; her hands and
lips moved swiftly, weaving the spells of summoning. Now
she called forth a warrior-maid from some wild mountain
land: a strong-limbed hawk-visaged woman who carried a
shield and a bow.

Straight as a young ash, curious and unafraid, the
warrior-woman stared at Eirech with bold dark eyes, and
when he bedded her, she lay with a dagger under her head.

Through that long night there paraded before Eirech
queens and highborn ladies, courtesans, slaves and
peasants—from all the lands where the winds traveled, from
every age of earth. And when Dhagha saw that he was weary
of these, that he chose more slowly, she wove her spells
anew: summoning virgins with unbudded breasts, and boys
from the ancient courts who were skilled in the subtlest arts of
love.

There were some who wept and hid their faces, shamed by
the curious pleasures that Eirech devised for them. But there
was no escape. They were trapped like birds in the net of
Dhagha's sorcery.

Phials, flagons, caskets lay scattered across the carpet,
spilling their fragrant powders, their honeyed oils. In Eirech
there had been roused so great a thirst for pleasure that
nothing, it seemed, could slake the fierce demands of his

flesh. Yet all the while that he lay with one partner, his mind raced ahead, thinking how it might be with the next. He was like a man who has sworn not to rest till he grasps the two ends of the rainbow in his hands. Always, just out of reach, lay the promise of perfect pleasure, forever eluding him.

And Dhagha whispered, "Perhaps you are worn out by too much beauty. One may tire of lithe limbs, soft skins. One wearies even of perfection when it is commonplace."

"A curious thought," said Eirech. "And would you tempt me with something more than mere perfection?"

"Let us say, with something more than commonplace. A dash of seasoning to the jaded palate." Her lids drooped over her grey eyes, her face grew taut with effort. From her lips there issued growling, bestial sounds.

The shadows ran together, gathering form and substance. "Behold," cried Dhagha, opening her eyes. "I offer you a monarch who lived before the time of kings—queen of the first and ancient earth."

Eirech stared with fascinated repugnance at this creature out of shadow—at the squat brown body, clad in the skins of beasts, at the lowering forehead and thrusting jaw.

In the act itself he took a curious and morbid pleasure, but afterwards his flesh stank like a beast's, and he cursed Dhagha for leading him into abomination.

"I fear," said Dhagha, "that what you seek is beyond my skill to conjure. No woman such as you desire has walked this earth, in any age; no man has attained such pleasure as you aspire to."

"Still . . ." and she gazed at him in a reflective silence. "There is one whom I have feared to summon . . ."

Again she closed her eyes, and she summoned to the feast a woman whose beauty was not of the waking world, who belonged to no country on earth that Eirech could name. Like a man in a dream he gazed upon that wide pale brow, those wise and gentle eyes set far apart in the lovely face. Ageless she was, unaging, in a gown that followed no fashions of his world—that seemed to be made of moonlight, or spider's silk.

He dared not take this peerless lady as he had taken the others, with neither her desire nor her consent. And yet she seemed to read his thoughts. She smiled, and one dark eyebrow lifted a little. "After all, it is a small thing you ask," that look seemed to say, "and to me of what consequence?"

Her love was like pure spring water after a surfeit of sweet wine, like the summer storm that clears the heavy air and brings the soft rain to the meadows.

Lying in her arms, in the quiet aftermath of love, he felt no sadness, but rather a sudden blinding clarity of mind and spirit. It was as though he had been wandering through dim, cobwebbed passages, and all at once the walls vanished like smoke, and the pure light of the sun burst in upon him.

And a strange thought came to him—to Eirech, for whom love had been a thing brief as a candle-flame, for whom women had counted no more than the red rose petals floating in the bay. He thought, To this woman could I cleave forever; with this woman might I find pleasure that lasted as long as life itself.

And he cried out suddenly in utter desolation. Not merely because he must die, for that comes to all men in the end, and he feared old age more than he feared death. He grieved rather that having found the hope, the possibility of perfect pleasure, he must, on the very instant of discovery, lose it. It could only be that the gods were jealous, blighting whatever beauty there was in the world, as frost destroyed the perfect bloom of autumn.

"Why do you weep?" asked the lady, and she used the sleeve of her gown to wipe the wetness from his cheeks.

"I weep because having at last learned to love, I must learn to die." Hearing them spoken, he was pleased with the sound of his words; perhaps they were even true.

She looked at him with those grave lovely eyes. "I remember," she said. "It is not easy to bear one's mortality. I was not sorry to put it behind me."

Eirech's eyes widened. "What are you saying to me, Lady?"

"In my country," she said, "there is neither death, nor sickness, nor decay. There life is perpetually, eternally renewed."

He caught at her sleeve, at her pale cool hands, pleading with her, "Lady, there is nothing left for me here, in this doomed land. There is no place I would be but at your side. Let me go with you, to your own country."

All his pride, his arrogance had fallen away from him. He was a man capsized and drowning, who strikes out wildly for an unknown shore.

She said, "You cannot follow me there, I must pass through doors that are barred to you." And then, seeing the despair in his eyes, she paused to consider. "On the other hand . . . it seems that the cleverest women of these isles have taken trouble to entertain you, have prepared feasts in your particular honor. Can I refuse to do likewise?"

Had she been mortal, with the flaws of ordinary mortals, he might have believed there was a hint of slyness, of mischief, in her smile.

"On the morrow," she said, "you must go to the place you call Chuael Lh'hainn, the Cave of Mists. There will I open a gate for you into my own country, into the land that lies behind the mists. Tomorrow you will dine at the table of Madhir G'havann, the Master-Builder, who is my uncle and the High King of that land."

He kissed her two hands, and wet them with his tears; and then recovering his composure as quickly as he had lost it, he began to think what he would wear on the morrow, to the court of the High King Madhir G'havann.

To his annoyance, the next day dawned cold and sunless, as dismal an autumn morning as any he could remember.

Shivering, he hurried along the wet windy beach; through his kidskin boots sharp stones bruised his feet.

The sea, glimpsed far out on the sands through the churning mists, was grey as slate, and angry-looking.

He rounded a point of land, climbed awkwardly over a tumble of weed-slick stones. As a sudden gust of wind ripped through the fog he caught sight of the cave's mouth—a black gaping hole in the fissured rock. He shuddered, and drawing his cloak around him, made his way slowly to the base of the cliff.

Within the cavern there was not the darkness he had imagined, but a cold grey gloom through which the mists writhed and coiled like snakes.

Suddenly panic caught him by the throat. He had not thought to ask when the tide turned. How long before the sea boiled up against the cliff's face, poured through that narrow opening?

He listened, heard nothing but the faint sobbing of the wind, and so he shrugged and went on, into the heart of the cavern.

Presently he entered a low narrow passageway, smelling of seaweed and damp rock. Underfoot the ground was slimed and treacherous; his boots squelched at every step. It was bitter cold in this place where the sun could not reach; a raw chill that gnawed at his bones.

What was that sound? Surely this time it was the roar of the waves, racing like a savage army over the sands, bent upon his destruction. His heart crashed against his ribs; his throat was dry with terror.

The roof of the passage swooped suddenly, forcing him to crouch, to shuffle. He went rigid with shock as a cold trickle of water ran down his neck.

And then, suddenly, suddenly, there was a glimmer of grey light at the end of the passage. He stumbled forward, and emerged into a huge vaulted room of stone.

Here too the mists curled and wreathed about him. Yet in

this place they had taken on a luminous, silvery quality; translucent, shimmering, they hung in the grey air like ribbons of gauze.

He left the cave, passed out of the ordinary world of men into a place that was like the summer dawn, like the many-colored inner surface of a shell. This landscape was curiously familiar to him—he thought he knew the outline of those hills, that curve of shoreline—yet all was transmuted, made strange, as though by sorcery. At the edge of his vision shapes seemed subtly and mysteriously to alter—to form and dissolve like mist. Or perhaps it was only the light that made it seem so—that cool limpid light that even at broad noon had something of moonlight's distorting, dreamlike quality.

In the near distance was a placid sea that shimmered like grey satin, and arching over it a summer sky, unclouded and serene. He could not tell the color of that sky; it glowed with a myriad of shifting, iridescent hues.

The countryside was rich with the coming harvest. The wind whispered, bees hummed, in fields of fragrant grasses. Birds sang with voices sweeter than any he had heard on earth. In the orchards trees bowed low under the weight of bright fruits that shone like jewels.

In this soft weather his cloak was burdensome; he threw it back, to reveal the new tunic of silver and lavender, the amethyst-studded girdle that he had put on for this journey.

As he walked through this rainbow-colored land, the light deepened and began to fade; violet shadows ran down from the hills. Gradually, over the fields and orchards, there gathered a soft luminous dusk.

Presently he came to a great hall of some pale smooth stone that gleamed like silver in the gentle dark. As he approached a blaze of light leaped up suddenly at every window, as though in welcome. He went in through doors of crystal, afire with mirrored torchlight; into the court of Madhir G'havann the Master-Builder, High King of this land.

A feast was about to begin; the air was full of rich fragrances that went like wine to Eirech's head. Music played softly; servants, tray-laden, moved soundlessly among the tables, among the assembled lords and ladies.

Ah, thought Eirech with satisfaction. It is me they are waiting for, I am the honored guest, the visitor from a far country. Before going in to be received he tugged his tunic carefully into place and smoothed down his wind-ruffled hair.

How beautiful they were, these folk that lived behind the mists. He marveled at the radiant clarity of their eyes, the egg-shell smoothness of their skins. He delighted in the gowns, as delicate as spider's silk, the gossamer skirts and sleeves of the pale exquisite ladies. And his head swam with the fragrance of flowers that bloomed everywhere, without regard to season, the glitter of gold and gleam of silver, the jewel-encrusted tapestries.

This, said Eirech to himself, this is the place I would choose to dwell. It was as though in his own world a pall had lain over everything, obscuring the true beauty at the heart of things, as tarnish hides the beauty of silver.

"Eirech. Eirech of the Silver Eyes." A voice, remote and hollow-sounding down the vast reaches of that hall; but unmistakable in its command, its calm authority. Eirech moved as in a dream among those shining throngs, down endless-seeming distances, coming at last to stand before a king who looked at him with eyes that were shrewd and questioning, yet strangely gentle.

"Your journey was long," said Madhir G'havann. "There is a look of hunger in your eyes, and I think it will take more than food and drink to quiet that appetite. What have you come to ask of me, Eirech of the Silver Eyes?"

Eirech drew a long considering breath. He was hearing in his mind the soft echo of a voice: "In my world there is no death, no sickness, no decay. Life there is perpetually, eternally renewed . . ."

Well, he thought, we are given nothing in this life save

what we ask for. "My Lord," he said, and as he spoke he could hear his heart thudding in his chest. "My Lord, I wish to live forever."

There, it was out, there was no turning back. But he knew he must choose his words with care. He was remembering tales of bargains made with enchanters and faerie folk: agreements that for the want of the right words were in the end no bargain at all.

"I wish to remain always as you see me now, neither older, nor less pleasing to the eye. Vulnerable to no weapon, nor to any wound that may be inflicted upon me. And above all, safe from drowning, freezing, burning, from all the hazards of the natural world."

"All this may be given you. But reflect well on what you ask—once done, it cannot be undone."

"My Lord, I have reflected. What greater gift could any man be given?"

"So then," said the High King Madhir G'havann. "You shall have your wish."

And from the watching throng a soft sigh went up, like a rising wind; had Eirech thought to listen, he might have heard in that sound a kind of wondering pity, and might have taken warning from it.

"And yet," said the High King, "there must be a price paid. You are born of a sorcerer's race. What arts have you, Eirech? What magic?"

"No magic, my Lord, except that I lay claim to one small gift."

"And that is?"

"The gift of song, my Lord."

"Then that is the price we ask."

"You shall have it, and welcome," said Eirech. He was doubly pleased. What artist would spurn the chance to perform on such a stage, to be applauded by so noble a company?

"Eirech," said the King, and something in his voice

brought a sudden chill to Eirech's heart. "You must know the meaning of the bargain you make. We do not ask only to borrow your voice. That would be a small price to pay for immortality."

All the color had drained from Eirech's face. "Why, my Lord?" he asked, in an anguished whisper. "Your price leaves me immeasurably poorer, and in no way enriches yourself."

"Eirech, in what other coin are you prepared to pay?"

He could not answer. His barge, his house in the Peony Court? The gold coins in his vault? What value could they have, in this land of inestimable riches? What value for anyone, once the sea had claimed them? His beauty, his youth, the suppleness of his dancer's limbs? Without those things, the bargain lacked all purpose.

He said, "So be it, my Lord. If that is your price, I will pay it."

And turning to the lords and ladies of the court, he prepared to sing his last and his sweetest song. He had left his harp behind, but it was no matter, he had no need of accompaniment.

He saw her then, standing a little apart from the others— that sweet pale face that he would know among all the faces of earth. She was watching him with a trace of a smile pulling at the corners of her mouth. He looked into her eyes, and his song poured from his throat like moonlight, like cold pure water upon the rocks. He knew that he had never sung half so well as this, in all the courts and palaces of the west, for any earthly king. It was for her alone that he sang, that pale lady whose beauty tore at his heart.

The song ended. He felt drained, saddened, like a cup emptied to the dregs.

"You sang well," said the High King Madhir G'havann. "Even in our world there are few to match you, Eirech of the Silver Eyes. Most nobly have you fulfilled your side of the bargain. Now I must fulfill mine. Bring me the Cup," he said to his chief steward; and the man went at once to do his bidding.

Gently, reverently, it was set down before the throne, that vessel that was the fairest treasure of Madhir G'havann's court. It was huge, so huge that two servants were needed to carry it, one on either side, and full to overflowing. No gold of Eirech's world had ever shone with so dazzling, so unearthly a radiance; no mortal craftsman had the skill to work those intricate patterns of enchantment. A strange flickering light played about its rim; one could not look too closely at that light for fear of blindness.

"Drink deeply," said Madhir G'havann.

Eirech bent his lips to the brim, and drank. So potent was that draught that his throat burned like fire, and tears sprang into his eyes, blurring his vision. The room melted into an iridescent, rainbow-colored haze.

When he came to himself, when he could see clearly, it was as though no time at all had passed. The High King sat as before, regarding Eirech with that grey gaze, at once benign and penetrating. The lords and ladies waited in a thoughtful silence, while fragrant steam rose from the golden dishes.

"The banquet awaits," said Madhir G'havann. And after this—thought Eirech, drunk with triumph—a thousand, a million banquets more, banquets till the world ends, and beyond.

When Madhir G'havann had at last retired and Eirech was free to stay or go, he sought out his pale lady and pressed close to her side. "Lady," he murmured, "this hall is a fair place. But how much fairer must be the chamber where you lie . . ."

"Truly, Eirech, your mind runs always in the one direction." But she made no protest when he asked her to bid the company goodnight.

It seemed to him that the pleasures of love, like other things in this land, were sweeter, sharper, altogether more entrancing than any he had known before. Or perhaps the change was in himself. No longer was he as other mortals. Eternal, indestructible, must he not be in all things god-like?

She turned on her side, his nameless lady, and looked at him with an expression impossible to read.

"Was that pleasure enough for you?" she asked with gentle irony.

"Lady," he said, "there is a song I have sung sometimes, in earthly courts, and never till now have I understood its meaning."

"What song is that?" she murmured.

"Surely you must know it—it tells of the warrior Khyved, who lost his heart to a woman of faerie . . ."

Lying back with his hands under his head, he began the first poignant bars of that ancient song—"In the whitethorn month Lord Khyved rode . . ."—and faltered to a stop, appalled at the gull's voice, the hoarse and tuneless croaking, that issued from his throat. Already he had forgotten Madhir G'havann's price.

He shrugged. "It is no matter," he said. "There is beauty enough in your world. Now that I have found this perfect place, what need have I of my art, that was less than perfect?"

She looked at him with sorrowing pity. "But do you not understand? Eirech of the Silver Eyes, you are human still. You must return to the world of mortal folk. There is no place for you in this world—as there is no place for me in yours."

"But you have two arms, lips, eyes. Your flesh is as solid as mine."

"Once I was mortal, but no longer."

"What are you, then? A ghost? A shade?"

"In your world, perhaps. I am real enough in mine—and in all the worlds that lie above and beyond it. For you must know, Eirech, there is not one world beyond your own, but many worlds, each one vanishing into the next like ripples on the water. They are mutable and various as the sky's colors, innumerable as grains of sand. All things must grow and change, even we who are immortal; and so as we learn wisdom in one world, we are thereby set free to seek a higher, brighter one.''

"We, lady?"

"Why, all those who, dwelling in that first and lowest world—your world—have grown in wisdom, and in the end have been set free."

"How, lady? By what means are they set free?" Though he had guessed the answer before he heard her whisper it: "Through death."

She sighed. "And that is the true price you have paid, Eirech. For you, until time itself shall end, there is one world only; and you must be content with it."

"Lady," he said, "this is a cruel joke you have played upon me."

"We gave you only what you asked, in every respect according to your wishes."

"And let me believe what I wished to believe. Well, lady, cruel as you are, I cannot endure the thought of life without you. If I cannot remain in your world, you must return with me to mine."

Gravely she shook her head. "We are not meant to live in the world of mortal men. To do so is to violate the order of things. I went there once, when the sorceress Dhagha called me. But she is wise enough, I think, that she will not invite me there a second time. I saw how she looked, when I answered her summons—knowing that perhaps this time she had opened one door too many.

"No, Eirech. You have made your bargain. This one night only, as my guest, you may remain." She rose and drew on her robe of gossamer silk, which clung like moonlight to her sweet flesh. "At dawn I will show you the way back to your own lands. Till then, sleep well. Take comfort in the knowledge that you have defeated death—and that is a thing few men have accomplished."

And you, lady, he thought, for all your gentleness and candor, your innocent look—truly, you have defeated me.

Dawn came. Through the windows of Madhir G'havann's palace the sky glowed with a thousand subtle colors. The beauty of that sunrise was like a knife twisted in Eirech's heart.

"It is time." Her voice at his bedside—soft and gracious as ever, yet with an edge of something austere, uncompromising. How beautiful she was in the clear morning light—and how remote. It was as though in the night an unbridgeable gulf had opened up between them.

He left the bright court of Madhir G'havann, entered once again that grim passageway between the worlds. Shuddering, he crept through those lightless corridors, rank with the smell of rotting weed, and seething with vapors that moved like chill insubstantial fingers over his flesh.

All at once he heard a whispering, rushing sound—a sound that might almost have been the wind. His stomach knotted into a tight hard ball; he began to whimper, deep in his throat. Presently, as the first wave of icy water washed over his feet, he screamed—a strangled, despairing wail.

A great roaring filled his head; the water rose to his calves, his knees. And then, as black seawater boiled through the cavern's mouth, he was swept up like a leaf, like a chip of wood, battered without mercy against the jagged roof. He felt his bones crack; his lungs burst. In time the currents dragged him down again into the dark tumultuous waters, and he drifted beyond the reach of pain.

He opened his eyes. He was lying on his face in the wet sand, half-throttled by his sodden cloak. He lifted his head, and salt water ran from his wet hair into his eyes.

He was alive. He turned over in the sand and sat up. He was stiff and sore in every muscle; his tunic was ripped from shoulder to wrist, exposing an arm livid with bruises. Yet moments later, miraculously, the pain had faded, his limbs had regained their suppleness and vigor. Even as he watched, the bruise on his arm faded to a faint yellowish shadow. "I live," he shouted aloud, and he danced a kind of jig on the wet sand out of sheer relief. "I am immortal, indestructible. The sea cannot harm me."

But as he made his way along the shore that brief joy faded. It was grey weather, cold and overcast, with a raw wind off the sea. Gulls cried dismally over the gaunt cliffs. He could not remember without bitterness that bright land, those blessed folk, for whom no winter would ever come.

Waiting in the Peony Court he found the ladies Dhagha, N'hadha, and Arianth. Listless and pale, they languished upon his couches, eating sweetmeats and speculating upon his absence. Though he had been in the land beyond the mists but a day and a night, in his own world a fortnight had slipped by.

They brightened when they saw him, ringing at once for wine and honeycakes, and ordering a bath to be drawn.

"Where have you been?" they demanded. "We are impatient for the song that was promised us." He did not answer. There was something avid and feverish in their eyes that all at once he found repellent. Never again, he thought, would he be roused by those soft greedy hands, those hungry lips.

Forlornly, he looked around him. In the melancholy light of afternoon his rooms seemed stale and somehow diminished. The luster had faded from the rich woods, the marble floors, the fittings of silver and onyx. The carpets and tapestries that had once glowed like jewels seemed, to his changed eyes, drab and colorless.

"We have not left your house in a week," N'hadha was grumbling, "and not one soul has called upon us. The poor fools are packing up their clothes and their jewels and getting ready to run away."

"Or trying," said Dhagha, "to calm the gods by magic. Day and night you can hear them chanting in the temple; the sound of it is enough to drive one mad."

"Eirech," said Arianth, pouring wine for him, "tell us which of us has most pleased you, to which of us you will give your song. We have been remembering, these past days, that when all other pleasures fail, there is still your music to make life endurable."

At that, he gave a shout of bitter laughter, so that they stared at him in puzzlement and alarm. "Never again," he said. "Till the world ends, you will hear no more songs from me."

"In that case," said Dhagha in a sullen, dispirited voice, "I hope that the end will come soon. I could bear it better than this dismal tedium."

And what of me? thought Eirech. He felt his heart constrict, grow cold and heavy as a lump of granite. "You speak of tedium. When all of you are drowned and I am alone— what shall I do for amusement then, through the rest of eternity?"

And he fell into a deep gloom, an agony of self-pity, from which they were not able to rouse him. Of them all, it seemed to Eirech, he was the most truly condemned. Soon now the courts and palaces of the Grey Isles would lie beneath the sea. Fishes would swim among the red pillars of the Peony Court. And what would become of him, how should he live—he who had slept all his life between silken sheets?

Must he flee to the wild lands? To a life without beauty, grace, or comfort—without even the consolation of his art? He could not survive there for a single year, much less for eternity.

Yet when he had sent them all away and he lay wide-eyed and sleepless in his bed, the thought came to him, "If I am truly immortal, if I can be slain by no man's weapon—why then, I can be refused nothing. Not even by my cousin Dhan . . ."

And he began to dream of the golden south—of the white towers, the luminous waters of Aprilioth. In those ancient isles a man could devote a thousand lifetimes to the search for pleasure. There indeed, in some antique vault, he might find a clue to the ultimate ecstasy—a scroll dim with the dust of aeons, a runestone lying in a cobweb-shrouded casket. Waiting for one who had sought it with illimitable patience through the centuries.

Can it be, he thought, as he drifted into sleep, that I have not made such a bad bargain after all?

Dhan was sitting cross-legged on the foredeck, polishing a spear. Shading his eyes from the sun, he squinted at Eirech—equably enough, though the lines that furrowed his brow betrayed a certain puzzlement.

"You're back, I see," said Dhan. His strong brown hands went steadily on with their work.

"But not to stay long, if I can help it. They tell me you are ready to sail."

"Tomorrow at dawn."

"I have come to offer my services."

Dhan smiled. "Space is short," he said. "A minstrel is a luxury we can ill afford."

"I have given up minstreling. I will man an oar, if I must."

The smile grew broader. "Cousin, I fear it would unman you. At harping and singing I'm the first to admit you have no master. But those are not the arms and shoulders of an oarsman."

"Looks may deceive," said Eirech, disliking the shrillness he heard in his own voice. "They say that our cousin Thieras has chosen to stay behind."

He was gratified to see the shadow that fell across Dhan's face.

"Too late," said Dhan. "Her place is taken."

"Well," said Eirech, "rather than stand here arguing, let us make a bargain." He put his hand on the hilt of his sword. "If I can best you fairly in battle—and if you live—will you give me a place on your ship?"

"If you can best me, minstrel, I will grant you a place out of sheer astonishment. And what if you kill me? What then?" His eyes gleamed with good-natured mockery.

"Then I shall take command of your ship."

"Well, then, Eirech of the Silver Eyes, I'm as fond of a joke as any man. You have your bargain. When shall we meet?"

"Now is as good a time as any," Eirech said, and he slid his sword out of its sheath.

Slowly, gracefully as a great golden cat, Dhan got to his feet. His sword leaped into his hand—that shimmering blade that had drunk the blood of a thousand warriors.

Eirech was no swordsman: though he was quick and supple, and had some skill with weapons, he lacked strength and a warrior's endurance. But he knew that Dhan did not take this fight seriously, and there, he thought, lay his advantage.

With a dancer's agility he leaped, spun, cavorted; was here one moment and there the next; all the while slashing out with random ferocity, hardly looking to see where his blade went . . .

With what seemed a stroke of pure luck, he slipped for an instant under Dhan's guard and grazing his shoulder, drew blood. The smile faded from Dhan's face, and as Eirech's thrusts grew wilder, a slow bemusement gathered there instead. That look seemed to say, "Is it possible this capering jackanapes means to kill me?"

"I meant this as a game, cousin," said Dhan. "But by the Sea-Mother, I think you are in earnest." And he began effortlessly and steadily to beat Eirech back. Finally, with one quick impatient thrust, he knocked the weapon out of the minstrel's hand and sent it clattering across the deck.

Eirech stood rubbing his arm; the force of that blow had jarred him from wrist to shoulder.

"Give over, cousin," said Dhan. "You have lost the game."

"No," said Eirech, and he reached out to retrieve his sword.

Dhan sighed. "Will you never weary of this foolishness? There are some of us here have work to do." And he began to play with Eirech as a cat plays with a mouse, driving him relentlessly around the deck. Exhausted, Eirech stumbled, lost his balance, sank to his knees. Dhan's sword came to rest gently against his throat. It was a gesture against which there could be no argument.

"Do you admit defeat?" inquired Dhan mildly. All his good humor had returned.

Sick with shame and anger, Eirech put his face into his hands, thinking, is this the gift for which I paid so dearly? Once again, those cruel folk of the Otherworld had tricked and robbed him.

And yet the sea for all its might had not been able to kill him . . .

In a gesture that was half desperation, half defiance, he jerked back his head and offered to Dhan's sword the soft tender flesh of his throat. Dhan's brows knitted; he took a step backward in surprise.

"Finish what you have begun," said Eirech. "Would you sheathe your sword before it has tasted blood?"

Dhan shrugged, as much as to say, "As you like—but this game grows tedious." He raised his weapon, ran a thoughtful finger along its edge, and then moved it with such gentle and deliberate precision across Eirech's throat that without doing harm to the muscles and veins below, he drew a narrow welling line of blood.

Eirech knelt with his eyes shut, moveless as a figure carved from stone. As Dhan watched, red beads sprang into the shallow wound, spilled over and ran down Eirech's neck. And then his eyes widened. "In truth, cousin," he whispered, "that is a piece of battle sorcery I would give much to learn."

Eirech put his hand slowly to his throat, felt under a film of wetness the smooth skin, taut and unbroken. A great sob wrenched his narrow chest.

"Yet for all that," said Dhan, "you have lost the game."

Eirech's voice was pleading, desperate. "Gladly will I share this sorcery with you—in return, is there not a foot of space you can spare me, the smallest corner of your ship where I may hide?"

"In truth, there is not. I have made promises to others I cannot break. There is little enough room for food and water—we will need all the Sea-Mother's help to last out the journey."

Eirech knelt on the deck, and tears ran down to mingle with the drying blood. Like a vision of doom he saw the dreary millennia stretching away before him. "What is to become of me?" he cried. "I cannot leave this place, and the gods know I cannot endure the thought of staying."

"Go home," said Dhan, with more than a hint of exasperation. "This fear that hangs over us all has unhinged your reason."

"Will you not listen? If you leave me behind I must find a way to die."

"The Mother knows," said Dhan, "it is not difficult." And he handed Eirech back his sword.

"For other men, perhaps." Eirech's voice had risen to a piercing wail.

"I will not do it for you, cousin. I have killed plenty of men, but never a kinsman."

"Curse you for a fool," cried Eirech. And snatching up his sword in his hands, he fell with his full weight upon the blade.

He screamed as a white-hot agony burst inside him; his eyes opening wide at the sheer immensity of the pain. Just before the waves of darkness rushed in upon him, he observed the look of astonishment on Dhan's face.

*   *   *

Slowly, his vision cleared. The pain was ebbing. Though he lay in a fast-congealing pool of his own blood, he could feel the rent tissues knitting, the edges of that great wound shrinking and drawing together.

Wearily he lifted his head. The last curve of the sun was sliding into a copper-colored sea. He thought, how many times can a man watch the sun rise and the sun set, before he goes mad and tries with his bare hands to drag it out of the sky?

Sprawled there on the bloody deck he wept like a thwarted child, for the thing he had not valued and had thrown away. Too late, he had seen that when all other pleasures fail, the final pleasure, the ultimate gift, is death.

THE
THIRD SONG

Dhan

i. Departure

The day that we sailed, all the portents were favorable: the sky cloudless, the sea a pale luminous blue-green, flecked with silver, the tide just turned and the wind holding steady from the northeast.

As for our ship, from the first she took to the waves like a hawk to air, a thing of grace and delicate balance. They know their work well, our island men. There was much art went into her making, and more than a little sorcery besides.

They had built her of alder saplings lashed with rawhide, with a skin of bark-soaked oxhide, overlapped threefold at prow and stern and dressed with sheep-grease. They had used white ashwood for the masts, and the heart of the oak for the gunwales, making her high-prowed and high-sterned, like all our island craft. A lovely curving shape she had, that put me in mind of a salmon leaping. There were eight thwarts, and a

sleeping-shelter aft, with space for seventeen. The mainsail
was square, and bore my sun-sign.

We sailed from the Sorcerers' Isle on that summer morning, and Ehlreth himself came down to the shore to bless her.

Yet strange to say there was small pleasure for me in any of
it—the bright weather, the sweet manners of my ship, the
following wind. As I watched the Grey Isles dwindle into
distance, grief seized me like a black-taloned bird, and held
me by the throat.

I have never been one to look aft, as the saying goes,
instead of for'ard; still that morning my thoughts were half in
another place, and when of a sudden a choice had to be made,
I chose badly. In the priests' house they might say it was
preordained, that there was naught else I could have done.
That may be, but for once in my life I let my heart overrule
my head, and the Mother knows we have lived with the
consequence.

We were already far out in the bay when we heard them,
those thin cries like the voices of children. But children do
not swim with such stubborn strength, keeping pace with the
ship the whole of the way. As they lifted their faces from the
water to call out I recognized them, and swore aloud.

One, Nhikal, was a distant cousin of mine: a man whom I
loved little, for all that he claimed kinship. The other was
young Ghierad. He was first cousin to me and to Thieras
both, of an age with Thieras. There was something in the look
of that pale, determined face straining out of the water that
put me in mind of her, and wrenched my heart.

Their arms flailed the water; their eyes pleaded with me. It
was plain that by now they had overreached their strength.
Even in summer the open sea is cold in those climes; it soon
chills to the marrow of the bone, and saps the will.

I gave the order to throw them a rope. That was the first
mistake. Better to have turned my head away, pretended to
hear and see nothing.

They sprawled on their bellies in a puddle of seawater,

sucking open-mouthed at the air, like trout. Still coughing and spitting out water, Nhikal tried to speak.

"Save your breath," I said to him. "You've a long swim back."

But by now he had recovered enough to sit up, and after a bit he found his tongue. "Cousin Dhan," he said. He had always had a gift for talking his way out of trouble. "Cousin Dhan, surely you would not see a kinsman drown?"

"It has naught to do with me," I said. "I told you before, plain enough, there was no room. Seventeen in the crew, and no passengers. Every inch of this ship measured out, every biscuit and water-jar counted. The Mother knows why you have taken it into your heads to come after us, but now you can find your own way back."

Ghierad pushed himself to his knees and then, with more trouble, to his feet. He was white as skimmed milk from cold and fatigue; his teeth chattered. "Cousin," he said, "we will work our passage. If we must, we will sleep sitting up in the hold. Surely sometimes we will make landfall, and take on stores."

"That may be. Or more like, we will all starve and go thirsty for your sakes. Do you remember what else I said, when first you asked to sail with me?"

Sheepishly, Ghierad's gaze slid away from mine.

"Well, since the seawater has washed everything out of your head, I will remind you. When Ehlreth looked into his sorcerer's stone, he saw seventeen on board this ship—no more and no less. And so I chose seventeen, Ghierad—chose them for their skills in seamanship, or swordsmanship, or weather-magic. Not fifteen. Still less nineteen. If I change that I will destroy the true order of things, and challenge Chaos."

And yet when they pleaded for their lives, and laid upon me the claims of blood, which no man can with honor disregard—when Ghierad looked at me with Thieras's eyes—I weakened in my resolve, and let them live. Could I have laid my hands on a coracle, a raft, a piece of driftwood that might stay afloat, I'd have cast them adrift with an easy mind. But there was nothing on the ship that could be spared. And so, in defiance of the Dark Gods, at the peril of all our lives, I let them stay.

The fine weather held beyond all expectations. The crew was in good spirits those first weeks, and accepted the shorter rations without much grumbling. Under that huge empty sky, with the calm green sea rolling away like a summer meadow, we were less mindful than we might have been of the cramped space on board. But it was I who counted the water-jars, and watched their number dwindle as the air grew hotter, and day after day slid by with no hint of rain.

"Lhaera," I said to our weather-witch, "we have need of your magic."

She glanced over her shoulder at me. She had been standing at the bow, lost in her own thoughts as she looked out over the sea's glittering surface. She was dressed in a loose light robe without sleeves, and I saw how brown her face and arms had become. Her hair, unbound, was bronze-colored in the sun's glare.

"This life suits you," I observed.

She smiled, and the skin crinkled at the corners of her eyes. "I love the sun," she said. "Still, you're right, it's time there was an end to it." Shading her eyes, she gazed up into the burning sky, and her brows drew together. "It would be an easy enough thing, if there were any clouds, to call down the rain. But as you see . . ."

She turned away and I left her to herself, knowing that magic, for her, was a private, inward-seeking art.

Some questioned my wisdom in taking a woman on so long a sea-voyage, alone among sixteen men. But we had need of her art: no man in the Grey Isles was as skilled as she in the calling up of the wind, in the spells that gentle the wild seas and make plain the stars. And I would not wish to be in the place of any man who laid an unwelcome hand on her. She is mistress of other arts, besides her weather-witchery.

(Come to that, I meant her to have company; and so she would have done, but for the hawkmaid's high-minded stubbornness.)

All that hot morning Lhaera crouched in the bow under an awning, pouring a scant mouthful of our precious water from one silver beaker to another; her hands weaving and her lips moving in a silent ceaseless rain-spell. The sun hammered down upon us out of a brassy sky; by afternoon a blue heat-haze was shimmering on the horizon. Sweat soaked the shoulders of Lhaera's robe and ran in rivulets down her cheeks.

"The thing is not possible," said Cu'haid, my second-in-command. "There is no weather-witch in the world could draw rain out of that sky. Better she should give it up and say a wind-spell, for we are near becalmed into the bargain."

I looked round at the listless faces of the crew. Island-bred, they were beginning to suffer in the steady, unaccustomed heat. The boy Ghierad, I noticed, was flushed and heavy-eyed, his color too blotched and unhealthy to be sunburn. Since the day we pulled him out of the sea he had not gained back his proper strength, and I wondered if he might be harboring a slow fever. I thought I must mention it to the pilot Jhael, who had some skill as a healer.

"Look there!" Jhael had appeared suddenly at my elbow as though in fact I had summoned him. For once, that long sardonic face of his revealed excitement.

I followed the direction of his gaze. There it was, dead ahead of us, three-quarters obscured in haze, but real enough: sharp peaks rising inland against the hot white sky, the blunt thrust of a rocky headland, to the west the gentler curve of hills; at one moment solid and unremarkable and then, when you looked again, indefinite, broken in outline, a place of mystery.

I put my hand on Lhaera's shoulder. "Rest now," I said.

"There is landfall ahead. We will soon have plenty of fresh water, and food besides."

She got up slowly, stretching the stiffness out of her limbs, and came to stand beside me. "I find this most strange," she murmured. "As a rule I can sense the nearness of land; I would have sworn this sea was empty for a hundred leagues."

"By the stars," said Jhael, "and by all my charts, we are true to our course. There should be no land anywhere in sight."

"Yet land there is," I pointed out, "and let us thank the Sea-Mother for it."

The wind, by now, had died away to nothing, and we lay becalmed. I gave the order to let down the oars.

Hour upon hour the oars rose and fell in that glassy sea, and we grew no nearer to our goal. Still those cliffs and pinnacles danced on the far horizon, mocking us.

Lhaera kept watch over the prow, her expression growing steadily more puzzled. "Surely," she said, "this is not possible. Can an island grow wings like a gull, and fly before us?"

"A trick of the light," I reassured her. "This heat-haze distorts distances. It seemed closer than it was, that's all."

But when we had rowed on through another weary half-hour and still the land seemed to hover on the far rim of the sea, I too came to admit my fears.

Jhael came out of the shelter where he kept his charts, glanced up at the swollen sun, and said, "This island of yours, Dhan—at first it was dead ahead of us, yet now it is leading us farther and farther off course."

"We have no choice," I said. "We cannot go on without fresh water."

Come to that, I think I would have followed it anyway. It tantalized me, infuriated me, drew me on like the smile of a teasing woman.

"Dhan," I heard Lhaera cry out suddenly. "Be warned, Dhan. There is sorcery here." She had come to stand between me and the bow, facing me: as if she meant to protect me, or to hide the strange island from my sight.

Though it was broad daylight still, a silvery mist was rising from the water, roiling and billowing all about us. It had none of the chill damp of fog, being warm and dry as the day was, with a kind of luminous quality about it. Ahead of us, that elusive island flickered, vanished in the haze, reappeared for an instant, and abruptly was gone, as though it had sunk straight into the sea.

Lhaera's face had turned milk-white, and in spite of the soft warmth that enveloped us, I could tell that she was shivering. As for the rest of the crew I scarcely could see their faces, for the mist lay like a curtain between us, silvery and translucent. But I could hear their voices, cursing softly, or offering up a hurried prayer to the Sea-Mother.

Sorcery it was, and for all our arts of sea-magic we had rowed straight into it.

I heard the soft rise and fall of Lhaera's voice as she murmured a spell to ward off maleficent spirits. I thanked the Mother that she was on board, for none of the rest of us possessed such arts.

Suddenly we had broken free of the fog and had emerged into the clear light of afternoon. A small wind sprang up and filled the sail. We glided gently forward through waters that were fathoms deep and yet perfectly colorless and transparent, like no waters ever seen in this world. Looking down, we seemed to be gazing into one vast unbroken crystal, utterly without flaw.

A very long way down we could see the fishes moving over the white sands: slipping gracefully among those fronded, many-colored plants that grow in the sea's garden.

"There was a city here once," said Ghierad, who was hanging over the bow. Sure enough, we could see in that world so strangely revealed to us, the towers and courtyards

of an ancient kingdom, crumbled into ruin. Like Lhaera, I
shivered a little.

ii. The Isles of Dream

"There is your island," said Jhael. "And not one island,
after all. An archipelago."

Scattered like a broken necklace on the sea's throat lay a
chain of islands, stretching endlessly away over the curve of
the horizon. Some of these islands, windward-facing, were
grey and craggy, with steep forbidding shorelines. Others,
thick-forested, had rank dark growth creeping down to the
water's edge: wild country, with a look of sorcery about it.
But leeward there were quiet harbors, embraced by wide
beaches of white sand, and green sea-meadows, starred with
flowers. Inland grew hazel-woods and apple orchards,
green-gold in sunlight.

The wind was gentle but insistent. Eager as a salmon in a
spring brook, our vessel danced before it.

What shall I say of our voyaging those strange weeks? One
day I will make a song of it, for there is not magic enough in
plain words, without music. There was a time my kinsman
Eirech might have done such a tale justice; since I have not
his skills, you must bear with me.

There were islands in those seas where all the meadow-
grasses, the reeds along the shore, made a sweet sound like
silver flutes, like a thousand harps strumming; where music
rose out of the very stones and the brown earth beneath our
feet. In those flowery meadows grazed enchanted sheep,
with fleece that shone like spun silver, like the winter moon.
In the orchards red fruit hung heavy as jewels on trees with
silver branches; the flesh of that fruit was surpassingly sweet
and tender, the juice intoxicating as unwatered wine.

Towers we saw too, of bronze and malachite; palaces made all of brass and crystal, so fiercely bright it hurt the eyes to look upon them. Walled gardens surrounded them, inhabited by great white swans. On the long lawns unicorns wandered, little-heeded and unafraid.

But fairest of all was the island of the birds, and there is a song that only the minstrel Eirech was meant to sing. I can see them still in my mind's eye, the flashing wings of scarlet, emerald, lapis lazuli; the air vivid with music, the sweet outpouring of those many thousand voices, each one as rich as Eirech's own.

All these things have we seen with our own eyes, and other wonders besides. For days we drifted onward, aimlessly, in sheltered waters, guided only by the languorous breath of summer, a sweet strange indolence fallen upon us.

Days turned to weeks, slipping like gold coins through our fingers. Always the next island beckoned, and the next; though none brought us nearer to Aprilioth. Beyond these sunlit isles was a world where seasons came and went; where, before long, summer winds must turn to the wild storms of autumn. There was a hard choice to be made—and I had put off too long the making of it.

I called into council those three that I trusted most: Cu'haid, Lhaera, the pilot Jhael. I said, "These islands are little inhabited, with fruit and game enough to last for many lifetimes. The crew have come to me saying, 'Why risk the dangers of unknown seas? What price Aprilioth? This is a good place. Let us bide here and be content.' "

"May the Black God of Kharkum take the crew," growled Cu'haid. It was the answer I expected from him, knowing as I did his stubborn unswerving nature, that would make no compromise with duty. There is not much imagination in Cu'haid, but in battle he is the first man I would choose to stand at my back.

Jhael said, "These islands have a strong enchantment on

them. It may be that the face they show to us now is not their true face.''

''Jhael speaks the plain truth,'' Lhaera said. Her eyes were troubled. ''Sometimes, if the light is right, if I stare hard enough at these green fields and orchards, they seem to waver a little, grow insubstantial. Then I catch a glimpse of something else that lies behind, beneath; something I do not understand, that strikes terror into my heart.''

We were drifting still, with the wind and current, through a maze of sheltered waterways. To the west was yet another cluster of low hills, green and welcoming in the sunlight; to the east a harsher landscape of grey cliffs, softened here and there with sea-pinks and the grey-green of lichen.

Just then a curious thing happened: we chanced to look up, all four of us together, in time to see the sudden flight of a gyrfalcon over those grey cliffs, ascending in a line pure as a brushstroke into the upper air. It was as though for an instant our four minds shared a single thought: remembering one whom not even death could turn aside from her chosen course.

It was Cu'haid who broke the silence. ''It seems to me,'' he said quietly, ''that we must go on now, or be lost forever.''

Thus was the choice made, and I felt easier knowing that we were of one mind. ''So be it,'' I said. ''Tomorrow we will take on provisions, and after that we are quit of the place.'' I gave the order to Jhael to chart a course southward, into open water.

Next morning we came to an island of soft low hills and flowery meadows, lovelier than any we had yet visited. It was high summer, the hot still air heavy with moisture and the smell of blossoms. The silver-green sea was quiet as a mill-pond.

We beached the ship, and with Lhaera and some of the crew I set out along the flat sands in search of a stream or spring. I was glad of the exercise. My sleep had been troubled, and I had wakened full of a restless impatience, in a fever to hoist sail. Too, the mood of the men disturbed me. Now that they knew they must leave, I sensed in some of them a sullen resentment that bordered on rebellion.

"This is a good place," I heard one man say—he and his comrade had fallen behind, and thought I was out of earshot. "We'll never find a better if we sail to world's end. In truth, it is madness to leave it."

Much of this I suspected could be laid at Nhikal's door. I knew him to be sly and self-seeking, with a glib tongue that might sway even such sensible men as these. I was sick at heart to see how the infection had spread among them. Aradh, the hunter Conn, Uhlain, Fergha—these were men I had hand-picked for their skills and, as I thought, for their loyalty.

None of it boded well for the times ahead. In the cramped space we must share, with naught else to distract the mind, the smallest grievances were apt to swell and fester.

Above the shore were grassy dunes, and beyond that a green lea fringed with open woodland. There were no roads, nor any sign of human presence. Unfenced, uncultivated, the fields ran off to the blue-green hills in a riot of lush vegetation.

Following a sound that might have been the chuckling of a spring—or a woman's laughter—we made our way through the deep grass into a grove of willows. It was dim and cool there, a green cave of branches; a place one might come upon woodspirits, or fauns. And so they seemed to us, those four that we found dreaming in the willow-shade: the two young maids, the boy, and the strange old man.

We stared at them, as one might stare at exotic blooms in a sorcerer's garden. The young ones had skins luminous and pale as the petals of night-blooming flowers. So frail and slender their limbs seemed, one feared they might snap off at a touch like winter twigs. As for the old man, he was like a piece of driftwood washed up on the shore—twisted and gnarled by the waves, bleached to the color of bone, yet curiously beautiful.

I searched for words of greeting, and they gazed wordlessly back at me out of wide dark eyes. Remote and dreaming looks they had, as though their spirits had gone to dwell in some far country. Disconcerted, I held up a goatskin; thinking that where willows grew, there must be water.

The attention of the older girl seemed to drift toward me a little. One improbably slender white arm lifted, then dropped as though weighed down by stones. I looked beyond her, and discovered a spring half-hidden among tall grasses.

Unexpectedly, Lhaera reached up from behind and put her hands on my shoulders. Light though her touch was, there was a warning in it, a restraint.

"Dhan," she said quietly. "Let us look farther. Let us look in another part of the island."

"But just yonder there is water aplenty," I protested.

"I mistrust it," Lhaera said. She sounded stubborn, and at the same time apologetic.

One of the crew, the warrior Farran, made a disgusted noise in his throat; somebody else groaned. I feigned not to hear, for in truth I shared their impatience.

"I have a fierce thirst on me," Cu'haid said. "Lhaera, lass, is there something amiss with the water?"

Lhaera looked at me, and then at Cu'haid. Her expression was troubled and uncertain. Just then one of the pale maidens rose, strolled languidly to the spring, and kneeling, scooped up a mouthful of water in her cupped hands.

"See," I said. "These people drink it without harm." I walked over to the spring and, filling my goatskin, took a cautious swallow. I knew that Lhaera was not given to nervous fancies. I respected her good sense as I respected her magic. Still, this water was clear and stingingly cold, with no taste but its own.

"It's as clean as the water of our Grey Isles," I said, "and just as sweet. Only water, Lhaera. Come, drink.''

She shrugged, but I saw that she hung back, not taking her turn with the others.

When the water-jars had been filled I sent the men back to the ship, with orders that those left behind should come and quench their thirst. It would be a long time before any of us again tasted fresh springwater.

When the last of us had finished Lhaera knelt down and sipped a mouthful or two, rising quickly as though she had swallowed something unpleasant.

But now our thoughts turned to our empty bellies. Beyond the willow-grove was an orchard, the trees laden with an unfamiliar crimson fruit. I picked one of these and split it open; dark red juice spurted out and stained my fingers.

I carried it back to the willow-grove. ''Is this good to eat?'' I asked the old man. He looked at me with his gentle, childlike eyes, and nodded.

And so we picked handfuls of the crimson globes, and devoured them greedily as children; the sweet pungent juice spilling unheeded from the corners of our mouths and running down our chins.

I do not remember falling asleep. I recall only this: that in the middle of the bright morning, with no watch yet posted and sleep the furthest thing from my mind, a vast weariness overtook me, as though I had drunk too much unwatered wine, or swallowed poppy-juice. Lhaera tells me that when, one by one, the master and all the crew collapsed around him, Jhael went back by himself to guard the ship, until he too drowsed off where he stood.

It was Lhaera who shook me awake, dragging me roughly out of dreams into the fading light of afternoon. I sat up, half-asleep still, wool-headed, my limbs filled with a pleasant lethargy. I yawned and lay back on the greensward, watching the light shimmering among the leaves.

''Dhan!'' Lhaera's voice was gently insistent. It annoyed

me a little, like the buzzing of an insect in my ear. I pillowed my head on my arms and admired the way the low sun was gilding the edges of the clouds.

"Sit up," Lhaera said. Not gently. I obeyed her then, and my head began to clear, though I still felt lazy and content as a babe swaddled in lamb's fleece, and as little inclined to stir.

The air was honey-colored, rich with light. Patterns of sun and shadow lay under the trees like scattered coins. Through those pools of green and amber light my thoughts swam aimlessly as fish.

"Dhan," said Lhaera, and at last the sharpness of her voice penetrated my dazed mind. "Dhan, you must get up. The men are sleeping still, I cannot rouse them."

I dragged myself to my feet then, and looked around. The crew lay sprawled everywhere, on the grass and under the trees. They snored like a hive of angry bees, and in their sleep shrugged away Lhaera's hands as, shaking them and shouting into their ears, she sought to wake them.

Eventually, with my help, she got them awake and on their feet; all but young Ghierad, who, lying with his head in a clump of pale, huge-petaled flowers, seemed more like one knocked unconscious than asleep. He stirred at last, and looked vaguely up at us.

"Leave me be," he muttered, in a voice furred and indistinct with sleep. "I dreamed that I had died and gone to dwell in the many-colored kingdom."

Lhaera looked at me. Around us we could hear a soft chattering of voices, eddies of laughter, a thoughtless, childlike gaiety. The wind was heavy with the fragrance of those huge pale blossoms. Below, the sea chuckled and sighed upon the rocks.

Heavy-eyed, yawning and blinking, the men milled uncertainly about, and I knew that they had drifted only part way out of dreams. How easy it would be to lose them again to the sweet seduction of this place.

"You have been trouble enough to me already, lad," I told

Ghierad, "that I will not leave you now." Heaving him up like a sack of corn, I threw him over my shoulder, and in that fashion we made our way back to the ship.

Indeed, there was not much weight to the boy—I had not realized how thin he had become, those weeks. There was nothing left of him but skin and sinew stretched taut across the bone.

I dropped him onto a pile of skins and he lay staring up at me, his mouth twisting in helpless pain. His great-pupiled eyes were filled with a dazed bereavement, like a child wrenched sleeping from its mother's breast.

"What now?" I said to Jhael. Standing in the bow, we watched the sun plummet like a great ripe fruit into a sea of liquid copper. Dusk thickened the soft air. "Our stores are low. We cannot drink the water in our water-jars. I swear, Jhael, these islands cling to us like jealous lovers."

"Then, cousin, let us stay." Silent as a cat, Nhikal had crept up behind us. "We have found what we set out to find—safe harbor in quiet seas. What more can Aprilioth offer?"

Lhaera, who had been listening, turned furiously on him. "And would you spend the rest of your days in a poppy-trance, looking more like a drowned corpse than a man?"

Nhikal's smile died. His narrow features took on a sullen, stubborn look.

"This place has much to be said for it, and there are others here that will side with me."

I turned away, not bothering to hide my anger. What can one say to such a man, of honor, or duty? Seeing that we would not be baited further, he sidled away into the stern.

All around me I could hear the men yawning. None of us, it seemed, could throw off that unnatural poppy-sleep. It clung like pollen to the eyelids and befogged the mind. Half-dozing on my feet, I realized that Lhaera was speaking to me.

"Will you see to the lad back there in the shelter? He is

running a fever again. Jhael is with him, but he calls out for you in his sleep.''

As I turned to go, she caught me by the sleeve. "I have not told you all," she said. "Two days ago I caught him returning his rations to the stores. I said to him, 'Lad, if you choose to starve yourself at home that is your affair, but here you must keep up your strength. If you grow thin and puny you will be no use with an oar.''

"And what did he say to that?"

"That he was under a curse and will not live out the voyage, so it is better that food is not wasted on him."

"The Mother knows he is puny enough," I said, "without such foolishness as that."

Cu'haid added sarcastically, "Would that his brother had half his scruples. That one must be watched or he will have the hero's share of everything."

I crawled into the shelter of sewn skins. The boy was awake, sitting up in the half-dusk and regarding me with sad, trusting eyes. His lower lip trembled. Such childlike weakness should have aroused in me not pity, but contempt. And yet I pitied him. So untouched was he by life, so ignorant of the rules by which men live, that I could not judge him as I judged other men.

His face had a crumpled, woeful look. "That was a happy place," he said. "Why could you not have gone away, and left me there?"

His words irked me, echoing as they did Nhikal's. Yet there was more here, I thought, than Nhikal's idle trouble-making. I was framing a reasonable reply when he spoke again, still in that forlorn and childish way.

"Cousin Dhan."

"Yes, lad."

"Have you ever thought that you must die?"

"I have known that," I said, "since I was old enough to know anything. Though some men take longer than others to puzzle it out."

"I did not mean that . . ." he started to explain, though of course I knew well enough what he meant. "Not someday, when you are an old man—but suddenly, in a week, a day, an hour even."

"Aye, and in a minute or a second," I said. "Lad, you forget my occupation."

"And knowing you might die in battle, were you not afraid?"

"Soldier I may be," I said, "but I am not totally a fool. Yes, lad, when I had time to be afraid, I was."

He spoke with his face turned away, as though his words shamed him. "I cannot put it out of my mind," he said. "When I am asleep I forget for a little. Then when I wake up it leaps back at me like a great sharp-clawed beast. I remember that I am accursed. I remember that this is the last journey I will ever take, and that I shall not see the end of it."

I looked around at Jhael. His face was carefully noncommittal. Fool that I was, not to have understood . . .

I have seen that look of terrible knowledge on the faces of other men. Men who rode into battle, knowing full well the precise manner of their deaths. For them, for Thieras, for this boy, the gift of foresight was a curse indeed. Myself, I would not send any man into battle, knowing he had the sight. And yet oftimes it is on the very brink of battle that such visions first appear. So must it have been for Thieras. Few warriors have borne that fearful burden with such grace. For certain, I thought, this poor lad has not Thieras's courage.

Ghierad's eyes sought mine and held them. It was like looking into the sun's glare, the dreadful intensity of that gaze.

He said, "I have heard men call death the Grey Prince. They say he is a warrior tall as two mortal men, and terrible of visage."

"Lad," I replied, "I have not seen his face. Nor am I curious to see it."

And then he began to ask all manner of questions that I

could not answer. It was as though something long pent-up in him had suddenly broken.

"Should a man die under a curse," he wanted to know, "can his soul yet find its way to the bright lands, or is it condemned forever to the dark?" And, "Does the pain of dying endure beyond the instant of death? Does the soul remember and grieve for its lost mortality?"

They were puzzles meant for a priest's ears, and a priest's learning; there was no comfort I could give him.

"Listen," I said, "you are not yet twenty. Journeys, battles, the love of women—those are the things that should occupy a young man's thoughts. Jhael says you have a fever—maybe that is why your mind has taken such a morbid turn of late."

I got up, and beckoned to Jhael. "See what you can do with your herbs and healing charms," I said. "And as for you . . . ." I looked sternly at the boy. "From you I will hear no more talk of dying."

What else could I say? I am a plain soldier, with none of a priest's skills. But I knew I would be a long time forgetting the pain I saw in his eyes, the sad unalterable wisdom.

It seemed for a while that the Sea-Mother had answered our prayers, for during the late evening the sky clouded over and by midnight a warm rain was falling. At dawn, with our water-jars filled to the brim, we steered southwest toward the open sea.

Through that morning the sky remained overcast. I misliked the look of those clouds—they had a louring heaviness that boded storm.

"I think," said Jhael, echoing my own thoughts, "that we may have set out one day too soon."

iii. The Dark Land

Surprisingly, the storm held off; though the sky, by mid-day, had a dirty yellow-grey cast to it. To the east, the clouds were grey-black and sulphur-yellow, and curiously disturbed as though by strong erratic winds, twisting and spiraling upward into columns and coiling serpent shapes.

An hour more, and the afternoon light had been swallowed up by a grey murky haze. In that unnatural twilight the crew muttered uneasily of fresh enchantments.

Though the air was dead calm, the sea—like the sky—seemed strangely agitated, as though some deep turmoil were churning up the waters from below.

The air thickened and grew foul-smelling, with a sharp grittiness that chafed our throats and made our eyes water.

Gradually, in the dim light, we saw a film of greyish-white dust settling like hoarfrost over hair, clothes, bedding, every unprotected surface.

After some time the haze dispersed, or settled, leaving us adrift in windless seas, with the fine grey dust seeping into everything. We swore as we shook it out of our beards and clothing, emptied it from the cooking pots.

I discovered young Ghierad crouched in the stern, dust clinging to his head and shoulders like dirty snow.

He looked up at me, wan-faced. His hair and eyebrows were as white as an old man's. "See, Dhan," he said. "It is like a shroud, this dust. An omen. It is meant for me, but it falls on every one of us." And having said that, he would not speak again to anyone, lapsing into a deep gloom that neither Cu'haid's threats nor Lhaera's coaxing could dispel.

The morning brought with it no breath of wind. The sea lay smooth as metal under a sullen sky. Becalmed, we bent our backs to the oars; so listlessly did the ship move, it was like poling a barge through weeds.

The men seemed lethargic, as though the oppressive weather had sapped their will. The air was heavy, moisture-laden; the slightest movement made sweat leap out on our skin. It was as though time itself had somehow congealed. We were like flies trapped in a vast pool of grease. But for the pallid yellowish light that glimmered on the horizon, the sky was an unbroken, endlessly dismal grey.

In such circumstances I could not blame the men for growing uneasy and short-tempered. Much bickering went on, though for the most part it came to nothing. For that we owed more thanks to Lhaera than to our better natures. She saw us through those dreary days with a smile, a touch of her hand on the shoulder, a wry jest; so equable herself that she shamed the rest of us out of our ill humor.

Then one morning we ran into a sudden squall, with strong headwinds that picked up our light craft and spun it round like a dry leaf, sweeping it a great distance eastward. Eventually the wind veered and died; our headlong flight ended as abruptly as it had begun. Bruised and battered but mercifully undrowned, we fetched up in shallow water off a bleak, forbidding coast.

A grim place it was, where no mariner would land by choice. Everywhere was grey ash, slag and broken stone; shattered walls and columns crumbled into ruin. This grey inimical landscape stretched as far as the island's center, from which there rose an immense cliff or tower of black stone, sheer-sided, glassy-smooth, its summit wreathed in coiling vapors.

We had run aground in sand, not rocks, and the ship had suffered no apparent harm. Our provisions, on the other hand, were dangerously low. Until these last weeks there had been plenty of fish, and even some birds that Conn the hunter had charmed into reach. But few fish lived in these turgid seas; the sky was strangely empty of birds. Our island-

gathered apples and roots were long gone; now we had only
our dwindling stock of hardcake, sausage, and dried fruit.
That and foul-tasting water, perpetually on short ration.

"Well," I said, pretending more cheer than I felt, "it's not
much, I'll grant you, but beyond here is a great quantity of
empty ocean. Aradh," I said, "fetch me those riddle-bones
of yours; we'll throw lots to see who scouts for food and
water."

"There's no need," said Ghierad. "I will go."

We all stared at him. His eyes had a feverish glitter; two
hectic spots of color burned in his pale cheeks.

"Nay, lad," I said, "that was not a call for volunteers.
Give me the bones, Aradh. We'll let the Sea-Lady decide.
Who first throws the water-sign, goes. Two men are
enough."

We took turns with the many-sided bits of bone, rolling
them across the wet floorboards. Star, Tower, Wheel, and
Sorceress; Wind, Rock, and Fire; the first time round the
water-sign stayed hidden, and so we started again. This time,
as chance would have it, the Fish came up on Aradh's throw,
and the others gibed at him for his ill luck. The bones
skittered on the boards. In that cramped space we were
breathing down one another's necks.

I heard Ghierad muttering to himself as he made his second
throw, and then he was staring up at us with a look of crazy
triumph.

Lhaera turned to me with raised brows. Still, the choice
had been made, and not by me. I returned her look with a
shrug.

"So, lad," I said to Ghierad. "Get on with it, then."

Laden with water-jars, the two scrambled over the side and
splashed to shore. Aradh went because he had to, with a
hangdog look, but in Ghierad I could see a kind of frantic,
headlong eagerness.

"What ails the lad?" Conn the hunter wanted to know.

"A touch of fever," Jhael told him. "That, and a bad

conscience. He thinks to make amends to us, for turning up where he was not invited."

"I've never begrudged him his passage," Cu'haid said. "But I'm sick to my teeth of his moping and puling. The lad has fallen in love with the notion of death. Can you not see how he courts it? He has grown careless, and uncaring—a danger not only to himself, but to the rest of us."

Lhaera sent me another of her small, secret grimaces. I think she had known all along how things stood with the boy; knew, too, that I had guessed, and that Cu'haid was close to guessing. But now she only smiled and said, "He's young," as though that explained everything. Linking her arm through the pilot's, she said, "Do you not remember being young, Jhael?" Her voice was teasing.

"I was never that young."

Lhaera laughed. "I believe you," she said. "What a shock you must have given the midwife, all that length of you sliding into the world with one eyebrow raised, and that wicked grin on your face."

Jhael smiled down at her. Some said these two had been lovers once, in earlier days. They put me in mind not of lovers so much, as old comrades, who have fought their share of battles together.

Their smiles died suddenly. "Look," Lhaera cried out, on a rising note of astonishment.

Part way between the shore and the black cliff was a tumble of ruined stonework, half-buried in grey ash. Perhaps once those broken walls and cracked foundations had been human dwelling places; now they had a look of utter desolation—abandoned, one would have sworn, these many centuries. Yet among those derelict passages a kind of life still stirred.

As we watched, there emerged from the ruins a dozen black-cloaked, androgynous figures, moving in single file with cowled faces and downcast eyes. Stooped and shuffling as though they bore some enormous burden of age or grief, they made their slow way along the shore; and there rose on the grey air the most piteous and dreadful sounds I have heard issue from human throat. Such a noise does the winter wind make, shrieking among the narrow mouths of sea-caves, or howling through crevasses in upland steeps: a wordless, unendurable anguish.

Young Ghierad had been standing rooted to the spot, staring with wide and fascinated eyes; seeing, perhaps, his own sad fantasies made real. Then suddenly, before any of us could think to stop him, he went stumbling away from us: drawn, like a moth to flame, into the midst of that grim company.

The dark procession swept him up, engulfed him. Under the weight of some immense, invisible burden, his thin young neck drooped between his shoulders. His voice was a frail reed-note, soon lost among those hideous noises of lamentation.

I could hear Cu'haid cursing beside me. "He is gone mad," said one of the crew. "Now we are indeed cursed, having a madman among us."

"Aradh," I bellowed across the stretch of water that separated us. "Don't stand there, man. Get him back to the ship."

Aradh, who himself had been standing as one transfixed, dropped his water-jars to the ground and raced after Ghierad. Seizing the boy by the arm he tried to drag him away, but to no avail. I have seen it before, that improbable strength that comes to mad or desperate men. Furiously, Ghierad shook off Aradh's grip; then, with an outflung arm, he sent the older man sprawling into the dust.

I untied my sandals and threw off my cloak.

"Why bother?" I heard Nhikal say, as I leaped over the side. "Let the young fool stay where he is. We can use his rations."

I bit back my anger, and thought, I will settle with you later, cousin.

Halfway between ship and shore, I heard a low hollow roar which seemed to come from somewhere deep in the island's belly.

There was a hissing, as of steam, and then came a great pounding and hammering, like the noise of some gigantic hidden forge. Moments later—as I am told by those who watched from the ship—the mountain disgorged an immense black cloud, which flattened and spread rapidly in all directions. For a time it hung suspended between sky and sea, a monstrous many-armed shadow casting a pall of darkness over the world. Then it began to fall earthward as though under its own enormous weight, releasing in its descent a rain of hot mud and stones.

Now we were engulfed in a hot stifling blackness, acrid with the stench of sulphur. It filled my throat and lungs so that I could not breathe; behind me in the thick dark I could hear the helpless choking and retching of the crew. All around us in the invisible sea huge burning chunks of rock were falling; we could hear the water hissing and boiling up like soup in a cauldron. Meanwhile, the sky was rent by great sheets and serpent-tongues of blue light, blinding in their intensity.

The fear with which one is gripped at such times is paralyzing. One knows then the true power of those dark gods, the Lords of Chaos, before which our souls are perishable as candle-flames, and all our arts as leaves before the wind.

The moments that followed seemed like many days. All directions were the same, in that impenetrable blackness. It seemed that Ghierad had spoken truth; that we would all die here, choking out our lungs in the stinking dark.

I heard Aradh call out to me. I waded up out of the water, and made for the sound of his voice. Sheet lightning, blue and lurid violet, burst over us. In that sudden hectic light I saw black figures moving. Ghierad must have seen me, for he stumbled toward me with his arms shielding his face; Aradh was still some distance behind.

Once again that ghastly brilliance lit the sky. Someone

screamed, but I could not tell from what direction the sound came. I looked up, and saw a fountain of flame jetting from the mountain's throat.

I clutched Ghierad by the sleeve of his tunic, dragging him toward me. I put my hands in the middle of his back, then, and thrust him as hard as I could toward the water. He staggered, recovered his balance, and stood gazing wildly about him. Cu'haid, who had come after us, seized him and half dragged, half carried him to the ship.

A hot blast of air rushed seaward, ripping at my hair and clothing. Planting my feet wide apart I breasted the wind, calling Aradh's name and reaching out to him in the dark. I heard him answer, and thought that he was moving toward me, though we were yet some distance separated.

Now there came a terrible grinding, rending sound as though the earth itself were being wrenched asunder. In the midst of this, I saw a great white-hot stone hurtling down upon us through the black air. I cried out a warning, but too late. The stone missed me, but struck Aradh squarely; as the lightning flashed again I saw him stagger and fall.

Out of the mountain's belly and down its black face there burst a towering crimson wave, an avalanche of living flame. Swifter and more terrible than the onrushing sea it came, devouring everything in its path. I started toward Aradh, but before I could draw breath the monster was upon him, and in a hideous instant had engulfed him.

I shut my eyes against the searing heat and against the horror of what I had seen; I turned and, blind as a stone, I ran. The hands of my comrades caught me up and dragged me to a dubious safety. The hot wind and fierce current bore us seaward.

Behind us there grew a lurid crimson glow, like cities burning. I caught a glimpse of Ghierad's haunted face. "It follows me," he whispered, through blanched lips. "My death follows me, and will consume us all before it's done."

Once into open water the smoke-pall lifted, so that we

were able to see and to breathe more easily; yet through that
day and the long night that followed, dense dark-grey clouds
eclipsed the sun and stars. We knew that the wind had blown
us a long way off our course, but how far and in what
direction, it was impossible to tell. While the rest of us slept,
Jhael and Lhaera kept vigil: seeking by spell and incanta-
tion to tear away the black curtain that hid the stars, or, failing
that, to plot a course by divination. The task proved hopeless;
those ash-laden clouds were heavy and impermeable as lead,
impossible to shift by means of weather-magic.

By mid-morning, though, the cloud-cover had thinned
somewhat and the sun broke through, bringing with it a sultry
heat. Now at least we were able to plot our course, but though
I set every man to the oars, we made scant headway. It was as
though there clung to our blades some thick unyielding substance, viscous as tar or pine-resin.

Cu'haid cursed and wiped sweat out of his eyes. When he
held up his palm I saw that his blisters had turned to bloody
sores. It seemed to me there was more at work here than a
simple lack of wind and current. In these waters, I thought,
there must dwell some malevolent spirit that sought to trap
unwary sailors, and bind them to its will.

Finally Jhael called out from aft, "Leave off for now, it's
no good. We have not gained an inch this hour past."

Crouched beside him in the stern, Lhaera was unwrapping
a long package wrapped in deerskin. "I suppose there is
nothing else for it," she said, "but to call up the wind."

"I wonder," said a weary voice somewhere amidships,
"that we have not already done so."

"Do you think it such a simple matter?" Lhaera retorted,
with an edge of anger in her voice. "I may have art enough to
call up the wind, but I am not its mistress, and therein lies the
danger. I may summon a wind such as none of us has
bargained for, that will blow this little boat of ours straight
upon the rocks, or swamp us."

"Lady," another man said, "I would rather die a quick

death than stay becalmed here, to starve and rot."

"So should I," said Lhaera. "All the same, you must understand the danger . . ." She turned to me. "Come, Dhan," she said in a gentler voice, "I will show you what I have brought with me . . . I thought it worth the little space it would take up. It was a gift from my cousin Ainn, who had no further need of it."

Carefully she drew back the corners of the deerskin wrapping, and lifted out a soft and subtly colored garment. There was a kind of reverence in her face as she shook out the folds and held it up so that I might lay it about her shoulders. Many months of painstaking craft had gone into the making of that cloak. It was fashioned, the whole shimmering length of it, from the soft breast-feathers of gulls, gathered by Ainn— over who knows how many seasons—from the grey beaches that lay about her tower. The soft autumnal hues of grey and white brought back to me a fond memory of Ainn herself— that gentle somber mien that hid such rich complexity of mind and soul. I knew that woven into that cloak with every needle-stitch, along with Ainn's wisdom and her love, was the ancient art of the weather-wizards, the power to summon the wind.

The men stared at Lhaera with trust and awe. When one, tempted by the softness of the wind-cloak, reached out thoughtlessly to stroke it, his benchmate whispered a warning; the man snatched back his hand as though he had touched an open flame.

"Leave me now," said Lhaera. Wrapped in the colors of rock and sea and winter sky, she turned and gazed over the stern, northeastward. After a while we heard a sweet sibilant chanting, that fell away at times to a sigh, a whisper, like the wind in branches, then soared as effortlessly as birdsong through the upper registers.

As she sang she began to beat the air with her feathered arms, like a great seabird flying, coaxing the winds, with that ceaseless rhythm, from somewhere out of the vast still air.

At first there was only a faint troubling of the sea's face. Then slowly, steadily it grew, became a soughing and a whispering, a high wild moaning. The wind-cloak flapped and billowed like enormous wings. Now there came a loud throbbing and pounding in the sails, a steady purposeful creaking as the vessel stirred its stiffening joints.

A great exultant shout went up. Lhaera turned to us with a wan smile, and the tumult grew. So have I heard men cheer a battle-hero after a hard-won victory, and I know there are few sounds in this world as sweet. I added my own voice to that joyful uproar. At that moment we were of one mind, united, all the bitterness of the past weeks forgotten.

Lhaera slumped, exhausted, against the gunwale. Jhael caught her and steadied her with an arm around her shoulders.

In those few minutes our freshening wind had built into a steady northeast gale—a boon if we could keep the vessel running straight, a grave danger otherwise. Hastily we pulled in the leeboard and reefed the mainsail.

The sails bulged, the rigging thrummed; the sea curled and foamed against the hull. Violently the wind hurled us southeastward. Huge waves marched across the face of the water, cresting and toppling in a mass of spume, threatening at any moment to overwhelm us.

Every few minutes a wave cascaded over the stern; the ship jolted and shuddered, and cold water drenched us to the skin. The bilges were full; the shelters and everything in them ran with seawater.

Cu'haid, at the helm, fought valiantly to hold our beleaguered vessel steady. Those same men who had cheered the first gusts clung white-faced to the gunwale, and prayed to the Sea-Mother.

Filled to the bursting-point, the sails strained against the ropes. Now the mainmast began to groan alarmingly, curving under the intense pressure of the wind until we feared that it might snap at any moment.

Somehow we contrived to lower the mainsail and lash it down. Relentlessly the wind in the headsail drove us forward.

"Dhan!" I heard Lhaera calling out to me, shrieking to make herself heard over the thumping of the ropes, the ceaseless clamor of the wind. "Dhan, forgive me—I fear I have drowned us all."

I pulled her down out of the wind and said into her ear, "Hush, woman. There was naught else to be done, and there's an end to it."

I was worried, true enough. A man would be a fool not to worry in such a storm. But they are like fish, these skin boats, bending and twisting to the sea's motion, sliding as sleek as brook trout over waves that seem bound to engulf them. I knew, too, that there was strong sea-magic woven into every inch of our hull. So it was, whether by luck, or magic, or by Cu'haid's sure hand on the tiller, that our vessel held her own in those wild waters—shaping herself to the waves, riding unharmed through the worst of the wind's frenzy. When the storm died at last, we found ourselves sick, bruised, chilled to the bone—but alive.

iv. The Citadel of Zarimath

After that, our luck changed. The current was with us; a stiff breeze filled our sails and sped us briskly on our way. Whatever baleful influences had gripped us in those strange seas to the northeast, we had at last outrun them. Here the waters were alive with fish of every kind. There was rain at night and in the early mornings, so that we did not go thirsty, and the days as a rule were mild and fine.

The sky in these latitudes was a luminous green, with a few thin cloud-streamers low on the horizon. The sea was filled with restless changing colors—green, cobalt, pewter-grey—shot through with golden points of light.

Rearing up to the east was a steep granite headland, guarded by formidable rocks. We had been skirting it at a distance for several days. The deeply indented cliffs formed many natural harbors. At high tide, in dead calm weather, a ship might safely thread its way among the rocks and reefs into one of those narrow entrance-channels. At present, with a strong swell and a steady offshore wind, it was a rash if not impossible undertaking.

Then one morning we sailed between the mainland and a steeply rising offshore island. In this sheltered passageway the wind dropped, and the choppy sea smoothed out to sleek, humpbacked waves. The tide was in—it was a chance that might not come again. Spurred by thoughts of fruit, fresh meat—maybe even a civilized town with beds and taverns—we dropped sail, and followed the well-marked channel into a small snug harbor, tucked safely away on the island's leeward side.

Out of the wind, in the shelter of the little inlet, the sun beat down on our shoulders; the warm rocks gave off a pleasant smell of salt and herbs.

We made fast the ship, leaving two men to guard her, and leaving Ghierad behind as well. Though his fever was down, the boy was still morose and unresponsive. If we walked into trouble, I did not want to have him on my mind.

We went up a steep path planted with cypresses, and then a broad flight of marble steps. Clearly, this was an inhabited country. With luck, we would be given a sailor's welcome.

Looking down, we saw that the tide was already on the ebb; our ship, now the size of a toy, was settling comfortably into the smooth sand of the harbor-bottom. Beyond the sheltering rocks the sea was bright, wind-silvered.

Crouched on the clifftop was a great square citadel of white stone, dazzling as quartz in the mid-morning sun. The gates of this citadel were of black oak, bound in brass: immense double doors, three times the height of a man's head. Strangely, we had seen no sentries, either on the walls or at the gates. While we milled uncertainly about, wondering whether to call out for the guard or rap with our fists on the wood, the gates parted and swung wide to admit us.

"Go carefully," Cu'haid muttered. "Who would leave a place like this wide open and unguarded?"

"Magicians, maybe," Conn said uneasily.

We went in, keeping together, with our hands on our swords. Within was a wide courtyard paved with white stone and lined with statuary. There was a fountain in the center, and around the outer edge a planted border with many shrubs and flowering trees. A pleasant place, well-tended, its fragrant coolness welcome after the growing heat of the day.

Hesitant still, but gaining confidence, we drank from the fountain, washed the dust from our faces. And waited.

It was a curious reception. Long minutes passed, and no living soul appeared. A gaudy bird twittered among the branches, the fountain splashed cheerfully upon the stones. There was no other sound. The statues, sole guardians of this deserted stronghold, returned our gaze with bland indifference.

Yet I was not easy in my mind. My scalp prickled; obsessively I twisted my head to look behind me—and saw others doing likewise. Another time, that clear sense of being watched would have cried out, "ambush." Here, curiously, I felt no danger, only that faint prickling discomforture.

I sent Lhaera a questioning look: her nose for danger was keener than most.

"I know," she said. "There are eyes everywhere. But I do not think they mean us any harm."

On the far side of the courtyard we could see a line of archways, leading off to inner rooms. I looked at Cu'haid, Jhael, and the rest, and shrugged. "Nothing ventured," I suggested, and with some misgivings, I led the way.

Still could I feel those hidden eyes watching—a calm, unwavering vigilance.

We went through the central archway into a vast interior hall. The walls were smooth white stone, in massive, nearly seamless blocks. Sheeets of sunlight poured down through high narrow windows. Emerging as we did out of the courtyard's shade, the white dazzle of the room half blinded us.

"By our Mother," said one of the men in an awed voice, pointing.

All around the walls hung tier upon tier of glittering weaponry—swords, spears, knives, battle-axes—not only in polished bronze, but in gold and silver also; golden shields and helmets, silver breastplates, some set with huge cabochons of amethyst, lapis, topaz, and carnelian; and harness studded with a high king's fortune in emeralds, pearls, and rubies. Above and between, wherever space could be found, were gold chains, medals, tunic-clasps, wrist-guards. Higher yet were banners and flags in brilliant colors, and tapestries depicting ancient battles.

Here were all the accoutrements of war, but like no weapons, no armor I had ever seen, so rich were they in jewels and semiprecious stones, so intricately chased, inlaid, embellished. I thought this place must be a shrine, a monument, to some dead warrior-king, for surely no living army marched with such equipment.

Just behind us a quiet voice said, "I see that you admire my trinkets."

I spun on my heel and my hand went to my sword. He had appeared as though by sorcery—a slim soft-spoken man in black boots and tunic, dark-haired, dark-eyed, with a grave spare face.

"Softly," he said. Smiling, he raised both arms with palms outspread, then stepping forward, grasped my shoulders. His hands were sunburned, slender and fine-boned, with a cool, sure grip.

"I am Zarimath," he said. "Which is to say, the Panther-Lord, and I bid you welcome to my palace. Next door in the banquet-hall there is food and wine waiting. What may I call you?"

"Dhan," I said, doing my best not to betray the surprise I felt. In truth, I was caught off-guard by this open-handed, unquestioning welcome. "I am called Dhan, of the Grey Isles. We are mariners, bound for the Tideless Sea."

He nodded, as though all this were known to him. "You have had a long voyage, and will have a longer one. Come, let us eat and drink, and become better known to one another."

Turning gracefully, he led the way. As we followed him through that splendid room with its glittering display of treasure, I could not help saying, "The army that marched in such equipage as that must have been a fine sight to behold."

He laughed. "Those were not taken in battle," he said. "They are gifts from the lords of a dozen lands, a token of their fealty. It was a pity, I thought, to lock away such splendid objects; and so I hung them there, where I and others might admire them."

"And do you not fear they will be stolen?"

His smile broadened. "Not here," he said. "You may be sure that within these walls they are safe enough."

In the banquet-hall a meal had been laid for us, and we fell to with good appetite. It was plain, wholesome fare—fresh fruit, cold meats, a seafood stew, fine-textured white bread. The wine was neither mead nor the sweet berry-wine we were accustomed to drink, but the full-bodied potent juice of the southern grape.

Zarimath did not eat, but sitting in the lord's place, he nursed a flagon of watered wine and spoke to each of us in turn. I watched him with some curiosity. His title suited him well, I thought. There indeed was something pantherlike in the precision, the controlled tension of those smoothly mus-cled limbs. He moved like a dancer, but naturally as breathing, without self-consciousness. The source of that easy grace was neither affectation, nor the habit of long training, but something deeper, springing from the ancestry that had shaped the narrow skull and the long light bones.

He questioned us with lively interest about the Grey Isles, and about our travels, displaying an excellent knowledge of shipbuilding, navigation and oceanography. He said that he had heard other tales of enchanted islands to the north— The Isles of Dream, he called them—though they were to be found on no charts, and appeared to drift at whim across the ocean's face. He knew too of those stagnant deadly waters that had becalmed our ship. Once, he said, there had been washed up on the shores of his own kingdom a vessel of antique design; the men who went on board in search of salvage wondered to find instead the bones of long-dead sailors.

Thus the conversation turned to the occult sciences. Zarimath soon exhausted my poor knowledge, and that of my crew; and so he looked instead to Jhael and Lhaera, whose training made them better matches for his well-schooled mind. Soon the three of them were deeply involved in problems of transmutation, celestial mechanics, the nature of symmetry and chaos, and other abstruse matters I am well content to leave to priests.

The meal was drawing to a close. Before the servants came to clear it away I dispatched Conn and Gwyn to relieve the watch, so that the two left behind should not go hungry.

Overhearing the order, Zarimath gave me a look of gentle admonishment. "There is no need to post a watch," he said. "Your ship is as safe in my harbor as any of my own."

But I am not one to leave a vessel unguarded in strange waters; so I smiled noncommittally, and sent Conn and Gwyn on their way.

Finally Zarimath pushed back his bench and signaled to us to do likewise. "It is time," he said. There was about him an air of anticipation, of barely suppressed excitement.

We followed him along a series of wide white corridors which led us deep into the heart of the citadel. The walls were hung with tapestries—vividly colored hunt and battle scenes; bright rugs muffled our footsteps.

At last we came into an enormous room, white-walled, white-floored, two stories high at least, and open to the sky. Slender wooden beams ran the full length of the room, throwing black bands of shadow across the floor. Between these rafters we could see blue sky and the hot white glare of sunshine.

In the middle of the great room was a curious arrangement of pillars, the purpose of which I was not able to guess. They were ranked like soldiers on parade, or votive statues—two parallel rows of stone columns, graduated in height, and descending like a staircase from the center outward. The two tallest pillars reached halfway to the roof; the lowest were half the height of a man.

Cu'haid opened his mouth to ask a question, but Zarimath shook his head gently and put a finger to his lips, cautioning us all to silence. In truth, the room had a hushed and holy air about it, like a place of sacrament.

Somewhere a flute began to play, a sound vivid and clear as sunlight; and then, answering, the solitary voice of some low-pitched reed instrument—dark-timbred, melancholy. The music went on like that for several minutes—the flute questioning, the other nameless instrument responding; the bright music and the somber, like two minds circling, touching and retreating, until they met at last and melded, in one exquisite soaring melody.

"Now it begins," said Zarimath. "Look . . .up there!"

We tilted our heads to stare. A very long way up, figures were moving on the narrow roof-beams. With leisurely grace they came, treading those high treacherous walkways as casually as one walks a pathway through a garden. I caught my breath as the first in line leaped suddenly from that high place, and plummeted; then saw him land, as a cat lands, soft-footed, sure-balanced, on the highest pillar. He hovered there for a moment, swaying slightly, then bounded away to a lower column, making room for the one who followed after.

There were a dozen in all, men and women both, in white hose, white tunics—all lean and light-boned, like Zarimath, with that same supple catlike grace.

Their feet, in soft boots of white leather, were quick and sure on those narrow surfaces. Down they went, from column to column to the floor, then up and up again, across and over, the tempo of the dance building.

After them came a line of black-clad dancers—descending, ascending, crossing and recrossing, pairing and separating: white warp, black weft, interwoven on a giant loom. Though it was beyond my power to comprehend, I knew there was a pattern there, an order complex and mysterious as the movements of the stars. Jhael saw it, and Lhaera, and perhaps were able to sense a little of its meaning.

Prince Zarimath spoke softly, as though he feared by speaking to destroy that precise and delicate balance. "It is the dance," he said, "of the darkness and the light, of the Snow Leopard and the Black Panther. It is a celebration, and a testing. Those who would serve me, must know the figures of the dance as they know their own souls. It must be to them like the movement of their breath, their hearts beating, the blood flowing in their veins.

"The white dancers are those who serve by day. They are the architects of my cities, the interpreters of my laws, the judges of my courts. The captains of my ships and the generals of my armies."

"And the black dancers?" Jhael asked.

"They are the shadow-dancers, the invisible servants of the night. They are my ears, my eyes, the knife hidden in my sleeve."

"Today," went on Zarimath, "is the changing of the dance. Till this morning, those black dancers wore white garments, and the white black. A man grows soft and slack when he sits too long in the judge's place. And by the same token I would not have a man wear the black too long, for fear it may pervert his nature, making him unfit for the world of light in which we all must live. And so those who serve me must learn the two aspects of the dance, the dark figures and the light.''

The dance by now had gathered a dizzying momentum: black shapes, white shapes, merging in a blur of motion. Suddenly the music stopped and the dancers froze with it, poised as delicately as birds in midflight. A great hush fell over the room; one could not hear so much as a breath, a footfall.

The lines of dancers began to move again, flowing smoothly from either side, toward the center. The first dancer reached the pinnacle, crouched, and sprang: bridging in an instant of astonishing upward flight the great gulf of air between pillar and roof-beam. Hands, arms, clung briefly to the beam, legs swinging free in space; and then with a single fluid effort, he was gone.

One by one the others followed, vanishing the way they had come. The dance was finished.

I heard Jhael's breath escape in a long sigh of pleasure and disbelief. Catching my eye, he gave me a wry grin; and as he often did, he made a joke to hide his feelings.

''So, Lhaera,'' he said, ''we will become shadow-dancers, you and I. It is a trade would suit us well. We will go by stealth into the courts of eastern kings, and steal their magic.''

Lhaera chuckled. ''When I was a girl, maybe,'' she said. ''but I fear I am past the age for it now. I have not been as lean as that since I was twenty, nor do my joints bend as easily as they once did.''

''It's true, our women train for the dance from child-hood,'' Zarimath said. ''And our men too. Still, I have known some to come late to it. If the bones and the muscles are knit right, and the will is there, sometimes it can be learned, even in maturity. You, Jhael, for example . . ."

Jhael turned to him with a startled expression. "I . . .?"

" . . .might become a dancer still. Your bone structure is right, the way the muscle attaches to the bone. If you are determined enough, you are not too old to learn."

Jhael shook his head, smiling. "But old enough not to try. Your dancers have a dedication I have lost, Zarimath. Or maybe never had."

"I don't agree," said the Panther-Lord. "If one wants a thing sufficiently . . ."

I saw that Zarimath was watching Jhael with a curious intensity, and it struck me then that something had been offered—a suggestion, an invitation? Jhael saw it too, and flushed a little under his tan.

"Well," said Zarimath. The thought hung in the air, and I could see that neither man meant, for the moment, to pursue it.

"Let me show you something else," said the Panther-Lord, and he snapped his fingers, once, not loudly. Like spirits called up from the dark land they came, from everywhere, and nowhere: soft-footed, mysterious, their lean black presences sudden and shocking in the bright room.

"Not sorcery," said Zarimath, guessing our thoughts. "Rather, the true art of invisibility—the power of conceal-ment. They are everywhere. Within the walls, behind the pillars and the doors, in the dark beneath the trees. Alone and unarmed, a single shadow-dancer can disarm, or if need be destroy, a dozen warriors. So you see," he said, with a slow and curiously gentle smile that gave his lean face a sudden beauty, "why I fear no thieves within my house, nor robbers at my gates. Why you need not be concerned for your ship's safety."

He snapped his fingers again, and the shadow-army vanished—abruptly as though the very floor, the shining seamless walls had swallowed them.

"Now," Zarimath said. "You, Lord Dhan. And you,

Jhael. And Cu'haid, and my Lady. I will show you my kingdom.'' He led us high up on the wall of his citadel, and higher still, and higher, till the blood sang in our ears; up dizzying flights of stairs, into a windowed eyrie: from there we could look down as an eagle might, over Zarimath's far-flung lands.

To the west and north, great white-crested breakers rolled in from the open sea. Eastward across the green and violet channel rose gaunt grey cliffs, scoured and riven by the wind.

From his island stronghold Zarimath's rule extended far to the north and south along that lonely coast, and inland, over miles of heath and melancholy pine-forest, over river-lands and cultivated fields. All those lesser lords of field and moor and forest owed fealty to the Panther-Lord, whose rule had brought both peace and wealth to a divided land.

The light grew yellow; soon the sun dropped into the glittering ocean, and the air darkened. The night chill came quickly, in this high place.

''Let us return now,'' said Zarimath, shivering a little in his light cloak. He led us down the endless staircases, to the lamplit warmth of the lower palace.

Much later, when we had finished supper, drunk much wine, and talked away the better part of the evening, Zarimath called for a servant-girl to show us to our sleeping-chamber. She was red haired, and put me in mind of a little ginger cat—lithe and small-boned, padding along softly on her slippered feet.

She took us into a long lamplit room, with many beds in rows against the walls. Though sparsely furnished, it was a spacious, airy place, with tall windows opening on a private courtyard.

The maid showed Lhaera to an alcove bed, with curtains that could be drawn for privacy. Lhaera seemed pleased by this luxury, but also a little amused, no doubt remembering those cramped nights on shipboard.

Zarimath had offered private quarters to me, and to Jhael and Cu'haid. When I explained that there was no need, that many of our crew were lords in their own right and that all ranked as equals, he gave me a puzzled look, but made no comment.

The maid smiled and bade us a good night. In a moment or two there was a discreet tap at the door. Fergha went to investigate, and returned, grinning, with three large jugs of Zarimath's wine.

It was a warm, still night; a huge pale summer moon hung low in the sky, with a ribbon of mist across it. Jhael flung open the windows, and beckoned to Lhaera and to me. I picked up one of the wine-jugs and followed him out into the moon-drenched coolness of the little court.

Standing at the balustrade, we could see down the dark slopes of heather and dwarf pine to a narrow crescent of moonlit beach. Beyond it were the thrusting shoulders of the rocks; and farther out a black wind-broken plain with a glitter of silver on it. We could smell salt on the air; could hear, far off and muted, the roar of the inrushing tide.

Jhael, I thought, was drinking more than was his habit; as a rule he was moderate in that, as in everything. Tonight his long face was strangely animated; his speech hurried and a little careless. Small signs, that a stranger would not have noticed.

We had been speaking of inconsequential things, as one does when the hour grows late and the wine-jug empty. Jhael broke off suddenly in the midst of some story he had been telling, and said, "Lhaera, this seems to me a pleasant enough place. Does it seem so to you?"

The question was an odd one, coming as unexpectedly as it did. Lhaera wrinkled her brow in good-natured puzzlement. "I have visited worse," she said. "And better." Her face sobered suddenly; her voice was entirely serious as she said quietly, "Jhael, what is it you are asking me?"

"I meant, is it a place you could live, and be content?"

She gave him a long considering look. "No," she said flatly. "No, it is not."

"But how can you answer so quickly?"

"Because this is a place for young men, and young women. Younger, anyway, than me. And because in that dance I saw, there was sorcery enough for a dozen kingdoms. They have no need of my small powers."

"Now," she said, "you have my answer—and it is my turn for a question. Has Zarimath asked you to remain here—to learn the dance?"

"Yes," Jhael said. His voice was steady, and a little sad.

"And your answer?" As she asked that, I think we both held our breath.

"Love, I have not given him any answer."

She reached out and caught his hand, holding it in a grip hard enough to bruise. In the moonlight, her eyes had a moist gleam to them. I had long guessed how matters were between those two; and I knew that my own pain, sudden and sharp though it was, must be a pale reflection of their own.

Jhael said, "It is not my decision to make. You are ship's master, Dhan. Till we reach Aprilioth, I am under your command."

"Then tell me why you would stay with Zarimath."

"Because he has told me what a man must learn, to be a shadow-dancer; and he is prepared to teach me. Here there is true order, with all things held in balance, and out of that perfect symmetry comes power. The dance is only a part of it, the outward ritual. Here they have learned mastery over air and fire and water, and the demands of their own mortality. They can endure great cold and hunger, can survive for hours—days—without breathing. As you saw, they can render themselves invisible. They have herbs and drugs that are unknown to me, narcotics and poisons they use not only in warfare, but in healing also. I grew up in the priests' house, Dhan. I know a great deal of science, and something of sorcery. But now Zarimath has opened another door for me, into a place I had forgotten existed.''

I never doubted that Jhael could learn the shadow-dance. He had the quickest mind of any man I have known, and the sharpest reflexes. There was a deceptive strength in that lean body, and a skill with weapons that made me glad to call him friend. He saved my life once, in the battle of the Black Hills—but that is another tale, from another time.

I looked at him, perhaps more closely than I ever had before. He was sitting hunched over with elbows on his knees and his face resting in his hands, his wine forgotten on the bench beside him. I knew that, like Ghierad, he was of Thieras's house, a distant cousin. All that family have the same look. Like hawks they are, black-haired, with those odd copper-flecked grey eyes, and an unstudied grace about them—a natural elegance. There had been times these weeks that some small gesture of Jhael's—the lift of an eyebrow, a wry grin, or as now, that attitude of tired deliberation— brought back an image of Thieras so clear and sharp that a lump rose in my throat.

Lhaera drew me back into the long dim room, out of Jhael's hearing. ''Let me tell you the rest of it,'' she said. ''All those years when you were off learning soldiery, Jhael remained in the temple. When finally he left it, Ehlreth said that only the Lady Ainn, and Ehlreth himself, could name themselves Jhael's masters. And in the star-knowledge, even they took second place.''

''Yet he chose not to be a priest.''

''You know him, Dhan. Like me, you have sailed with him, fought beside him. You know the restless spirit that is in him. Can you imagine him living out his life as the priests do, in those dusty corridors, his eyes growing dim over maps and charts? As long as I have known him, he has hungered after knowledge. He will not be content with knowing what other men know.''

She turned to the window, looked out into the vast and

luminous summer night. "I remember, when we were children, a traveler from across the Narrow Sea told us tales of a far eastern land, where sorcerers lived—men who had learned to fly like birds. Always after that, Jhael swore that he too would learn to fly. He truly believed that the art was there, in all of us, and if one wished badly enough to fly, the magic would come. Then one day Ainn had to pull him back from the edge of a sea-cliff, where he was getting ready to put the theory to the test. And you see," she said simply, "what Zarimath's dancers did today, was near enough to flying."

When we went outside again Jhael's mood seemed to have lifted; he looked up at us with a quizzical smile. "So, you two—have you decided my fate?"

I said, "If it is your decision to stay, I will release you. Though I will not do so with a light heart, or an easy mind."

I was not ready for the look that came into his eyes then, that sudden rush of joy and gratitude. He drew a long breath, stood up slowly, and making a small ceremony of it, embraced us both. I saw him whisper something in Lhaera's ear, before he let her go. Whatever it was, it brought a smile to her face. To me he said gravely, "Someday, Dhan, I will follow you to Aprilioth, and I promise I will share with you all that I have learned here." He grinned. "Or maybe before then you will come looking for me."

Soon after, I went indoors. As sometimes happens, the wine had made me melancholy. Some men part with comrades—aye, and with lovers, come to that—as easily as they find them. For me, it has never been an easy thing.

The hour was late; by now most of the crew were soundly asleep. Most, but not all. As I fumbled my way to bed, I heard someone whispering across the narrow space between two pallets.

"There are more riches here," the voice said, "than a man could spend in twenty lifetimes. Having so many treasures, do you think Zarimath takes heed of any particular one?"

My temper flared. I reached out and seized Nhikal by the

long hair that he wore dangling in a braid, and wrenched him half out of his bed. Tightening my grip, I put my mouth close to his ear and pitched my voice low.

"There is no creature more to be despised," I said, "than one who robs a hearth-friend. Such a man I would strike down, as quickly as I would kill a scorpion on my door-sill."

He stared at me, his face blank as a mask. The whites of his eyes glittered in the candlelight.

"Remember that," I said, and let him drop. His head struck the edge of the bed with a muffled thud.

He had a gift for rousing my anger, that one. I was a long time falling asleep.

In the morning we made ready to sail. The crew was in good spirits after a night of shore leave, and I felt my own heavy mood lift with the brightness of the day. With Jhael gone, Cu'haid would have to take over the pilot's duties; but he had sailed before, and knew how to read the stars, so I had no particular fears on that score.

Cu'haid and the men had gone down to the harbor, to begin stowing the food and wine that Zarimath had given us out of his own stores. As for me and for Lhaera, we had our farewells to make.

The parting with Jhael was quickly over. I clasped his hand for luck's sake, and left Lhaera to say the rest.

Zarimath was in no hurry to say good-bye. "I will walk down to the harbor with you," he said. "I am curious to see this skin-boat of yours."

To reach the outer gates, we had first to pass through the Great Hall, with its glittering weight of treasure. As we entered, I spotted a man loitering by the further door. It was Nhikal—and recognizing him, I felt a sharp twinge of pre-monition. I shouted a warning. My voice sounded hollow and harsh in that huge echoing space.

I saw Nhikal's hand slide under his cloak—a movement so quick my eye was scarcely aware of it. But Zarimath missed nothing. His expression remained as equable as ever, but suddenly there was a chill brittle quality to that calm, like thin ice over deep lake water.

The muscles of his arms and thighs, the cords of his neck sprang up in sudden definition. He raised his arm. It was an unhurried, casual-seeming gesture.

I heard the air crackle like torn paper; smelled that strange sharp odor one associates with thunder. Suddenly, across the length of that enormous room, there leaped a bolt of living flame. Straight and sure as an arrow it went, like an arrow lifting and curving a little in its flight.

Nhikal started to raise his hands to his chest, and he screamed, once. There was a sudden stench of charred fabric and flesh. The scream was abruptly cut off, hanging frozen in the air.

I looked down at Nhikal. He lay sprawled with his mouth open as though he were still screaming, silently. I felt a little sick, seeing what was left of him. But no man could have denied the justice of the act.

Zarimath had come up quietly behind me. "Go," he said. "Take away your dead." He sounded tired and dispirited.

Hearing Nhikal scream, Jhael had followed us into the room, with Lhaera close behind him; now both of them stood dumbstruck, staring at the body.

"Go, Jhael," the Panther-Lord said quietly. "Go with the rest. You have brought disorder into my house; it is an infection that spreads faster than any fever-sickness."

Seeing the stricken look on Jhael's face, I tried to plead on his behalf, though I could see the hopelessness of it. I was glad it was not our lives I was pleading for.

"He has no part in this," I said. "If there is any fault beside Nhikal's own, it is mine, as ship's master."

Zarimath answered with a kind of sad, flat finality. "I have said nothing of fault. Who is to blame, or not to blame— what does it matter? Where the Lords of Chaos have entered,

nothing escapes their reach. Leave my house, that I may shut
my gates against them.''

We left the citadel, Jhael and I carrying Nhikal's body
between us, Lhaera following. Jhael had the look of a man
condemned—for some obscure and unremembered crime—
to a punishment beyond his understanding.

By rights Nhikal should have had a sailor's burial, but I
would not tempt the gods by taking his body on board. And so
we buried him instead in the sand at the foot of the cliff; it was
the only thing that we could do.

v. The Queen of the Silver Bow

On the third day out, a stiff wind blew up from the northeast, carrying us out of sight of land. Cu'haid, at the helm,
steered us steadily before the gale, our skin-boat pitching and
rolling as wave after enormous wave heaved up behind us.
The sky was low and overcast, promising heavier weather to
come.

In spite of this, the crew was in good spirits. With Nhikal's
death it seemed that harmony had been restored among us.
We were again seventeen fellow-voyagers, sworn to a common purpose.

Seventeen, I have said. The eighteenth, the boy Ghierad,
remained to us all a sad enigma. Dull-eyed and listless,
seldom speaking, he was near useless at the oars or at any
other task assigned to him.

Left to himself in Zarimath's harbor, he had brightened a
little: stirring himself to mend ropes and grease the hull. But
with Nhikal's death he had fallen again into deep melancholy. I had seen him watching by the ship as we buried

Nhikal; his face was ashen. It did not take much imagination
to guess what was in his mind.

All the same, he was one only, out of many. Sorry though I
was for him, there were other matters that demanded my
attention.

For some days we had been beating steadily to the southwest; now once again we carhe in sight of land. Jhael told us
that we had crossed a great bay, or sea, and the farther shore
had curved around to meet us.

We rounded a cape and sailed south again. To the west was
open sea; to the east a long steep coast of dark grey and
copper-colored cliffs.

These were treacherous seas, with high tides and strong
sudden winds. Near the coast the water boiled like milk over
mist-covered reefs. It needed all of Cu'haid's skill, and
Jhael's, to keep us from capsizing on the rocks.

We were two weeks along that coast, much of it running
downwind under full sail. Meantime we lived well, adding an
abundance of fresh fish to Zarimath's bounty.

At the end of the second week we rounded a great storm-
battered headland, with wild seas raging at its base. A grim
passage we had around that towering wall of rock: lashed by
the full force of the sea wind, twisted and turned by crosswise
currents. The crash of the breakers on the rocks was like
thunder, near to deafening.

Beyond that first bleak headland there reared a second
massive wall; but I could see now that the Sea-Mother smiled
upon us, for between the twin promontories there opened out
a wide well-sheltered bay, offering safe harbor. The waters
here were warm and near-transparent, with smooth white
beaches rising gently into red sandcliffs. The sky, of limitless
height, was a pure luminous azure; the sun leaped back at us
from white sands that dazzled the eye like snow.

As we beached the ship the men tore off their salt-stiffened
garments and leaped, shouting, into the warm sea. I took
Lhaera's arm and we splashed our way to shore.

"Fresh water," Lhaera pointed out. She was looking up the beach, to where a dense growth of cane and bulrushes marked the course of a stream. Suddenly she tilted her head to one side, listening, and looked at me with raised brows. Her hearing was always more acute than mine. A moment later my own ears caught the sound of a hunter's horn, high and thin with distance.

Presently three riders appeared along the top of a low red cliff, moving through a mist of sea-daffodils, with the bright blue sky behind them. As they rode down through the dunes we saw that all three were women: young and comely, slender as boys, with horns slung round their necks and bows across their backs.

Bare-armed, bare-legged, they each wore a tunic of dark blue silk with a fine silver thread running through it. White silk scarves tied back their dark hair; on their feet were sandals of white leather.

Lhaera's hand tightened on my sleeve, and her eyes widened. "How beautiful they are . . ." she whispered. I did not ask whether she meant the riders, or their beasts. Indeed, the animals they rode were as lovely as creatures out of legend: slender-legged, long-necked animals with a silvery sheen to their white hides, and a single silver horn springing out of their foreheads, above their large, liquid, gentle eyes.

The first rider looked at us. Striking eyes she had too, dark and long-lashed, with an odd upward tilt to them; but I did not take so much to their expression, which was cool and a touch sardonic. Here, I thought, is a lady who has a great deal of wit, but is not very good-natured.

Her companions, who hung back a little, as though out of shyness or natural caution, had a sweeter-tempered look; or maybe it was only that they were younger, and less sure of themselves.

"I am Razzan, and I bid you welcome," said the dark-eyed lady, in a cool careful voice without much friendliness in it. With that she wheeled her mount, beckoning to us to follow. When none of us moved, she looked back and waved an impatient arm. Her face was tight and angry-looking.

"I bid you welcome," she repeated, as though we were too slow-witted to understand—as perhaps we were, at that moment. "Our lady mother, the queen, is waiting. She has ordered a feast prepared for you, which will grow cold if you delay, and your beds are being aired for you."

I looked at Lhaera, and she at me. The rest of the crew had their thoughts writ clear on their brows. Still, I hesitated. Seldom did queens, in my experience, invite to their tables such ragged strangers as ourselves.

I drew Lhaera a little distance down the beach, out of easy earshot. "Listen," I said to her, "I know you have some gift for reading thoughts."

"Not thoughts," she replied. "That is beyond my poor skill. Motives, maybe, or intentions."

"Just so. And what intentions do you read here? Among strangers, I am mindful always of a trap."

"I have noticed that," she said, smiling. "Still, I see no harm in these women. No harm in the way you mean. And yet . . ." Her brow furrowed. "And yet there is a hint of something strange."

"Of danger?"

She shook her head. "Not danger. There is no hurt intended. But that older one has not much love for us."

"That much is clear to me," I said.

"Of her own accord, she would bid us depart, and quickly. She is following orders, I think."

Cu'haid, meanwhile, had followed us down the beach. "Clean sheets," he remarked, "and hot food, would not come amiss."

"I am of two minds as to whether we should go, or stay," I said.

"Go," said Cu'haid. "Take Lhaera, and the rest. The Mother knows they have earned it. I will stand guard until you send to relieve me. Jhael also. Though there is one favor we would ask.''

I raised an eyebrow.

"This time take young Ghierad with you," he said. "We have had a bellyful of his woebegone looks.''

"Done,'' I said. "Maybe the company of ladies will give him an interest in life.'' Though in truth I knew there was not much hope of it.

We made a strange procession: the three princesses in their rich boys' garb, on their shining beasts, and then a long line of wind-burned, seaworn men—and one woman—in ragged, grimy garments.

We crossed a salt-marsh, loud with sea-birds—gulls, plovers, lapwings; then up over the sandy cliffs, onto dry flat fields of gorse and stone-pines. Below was the headland: white and grey boulders studding brick-red clay, and beyond, the pale glitter of the sea. It was a land almost without color in that dry vivid light.

Higher up, the country blossomed suddenly with the amethyst heads of thistle and wild artichoke. Jutting everywhere from the reddish soil were grey rocks, over-grown with stonecrop.

The afternoon was waning, the light growing softer, with a hint of gold. We were climbing steadily now, through dun-colored hills; and then all at once we had left the dry stony fields for verdant, richly forested country. Here there were dense stands of oak and pine, and along the banks of streams, pleasant alder and willow groves that put us wistfully in mind of home.

Now, through the trees, we caught a glimpse of many-windowed walls and delicate towers; a roof covered all in glazed, bronze-colored tiles, so that catching the rays of the late sun, it seemed enveloped in flame.

We walked, in that soft thick light, along a road lined with oleanders, a mass of pink and snow-white bloom. Around us lay the palace gardens—long sloping lawns and shaded walkways, stone arches, peacock runs, an ornamental lake overhung with willows.

The riders dismounted; servants appeared to lead away their beasts. We entered the palace through great doors of beaten copper, framed in oak. The hall in which we now found ourselves was high-ceilinged, elegantly proportioned, filled with subtle, shifting light.

The walls were of parquetry—pale ash, and some dark exotic wood; the high narrow windows glazed with many small panes of tinted crystal—topaz, rose-quartz, amethyst, lapis. The light, falling aslant through those jeweled embrasures, lay in many-colored squares upon the floor.

A servant came and led us away to a bath of rose-veined marble, where there was perfumed soap and water running warm from copper pipes. An army of slippered servants handed us soft towels, and afterwards robes and sandals; a harper played to us while we bathed.

After that there was wine in jewel-encrusted cups, a board laden with partridge, rabbit, honey-glazed fruits and almond cakes in silver dishes, golden-crusted bread.

"Well," said Lhaera, licking her fingers and stretching luxuriantly, "I have nothing but good to say of this place." She was wearing a robe of some dark green fabric, which suited her well. Her coppery hair fell loose about her shoulders. She seemed rested, and in high spirits. Her face, under its deep tan, was flushed a little with wine; it gave her a younger, softer look. I remembered that in her day this quiet clever woman had been a great beauty, courted by half the princes of the Grey Isles.

I looked down the table at Ghierad, hoping he might have been cheered by the novelty of his surroundings. But he was slumped in a corner, picking at his food without any sign of appetite, and looking as wan and forlorn as ever.

"Lhaera," I said, "among your many arts, have you the gift of foreknowledge?"

"I suppose I have kept a little of it," she said. "After all, it is not a thing that is easily gotten rid of, like warts, or one's maidenhead."

That was her way, always, as it was Jhael's—to answer a sober question with a jest.

"Then tell me what you see for young Ghierad. Is it what he sees for himself?"

The smile faded abruptly from her eyes. "I have not made it my business to look into any man's future," she said. "And if ever I should see what I was not meant to see, I will keep my counsel."

And then she took both my hands and laid her cheek to them. "Ah, Dhan," she said, "forgive me, I should bite off my tongue for those words. You know that I love you dearly, and you must pay me no mind when I speak in such a fashion."

She knew, we both knew, that my question had been answered.

Until then we had seen only servants. But as the meal drew to a close, a tall graceful woman entered the room. Dark-eyed, dark-haired, she wore a simple gown of white silk, bound at the waist by a silver girdle, with her hair caught high on her head in a silver net.

She was not beautiful in the ordinary way, having a rather long pale face, and a high curving brow, with a certain sternness about the mouth, almost a frowning look. Nor was she young. From the youthful smoothness of her skin and her supple figure, one might at first have supposed so, but there was a grave authority in her look, a quiet dignity of bearing, that betrayed her years. That and a tracery of small lines about her eyes—an almost invisible web.

"I am Queen Zaidh," she said. "Happy am I to greet you. My house is your house. Eat, drink. There is plenty for all."

How curious it was, I reflected, that in all our travels we had met such graciousness, such open-handed generosity. Yet there had always been a price exacted. And so it was here, too, though I did not know it yet.

A harper followed her in, and a boy with a flute, and after that the three dark-eyed daughters, who had changed to women's garb, and several younger maids besides.

Then the music began; Queen Zaidh and all her court sat listening in a pensive silence, while servants came and went with wine and trays of sweetmeats. From time to time the queen would acknowledge an especially intricate passage, showing her pleasure with a quick smile, an inclination of her chin.

The musicians laid down their instruments. I felt a soft touch on my arm and, turning, saw the queen regarding me in that pensive way of hers.

"Your hair is the color of the sun," she said. "We do not often see folk with yellow hair. In your country—are there many with hair like that?"

"A few," I told her. "Though most folk are dark. I've been told I must have barbarian blood. There are savage folk who live far to the north and east of my country, in the wild lands over-water—they are yellow-haired like me, and warlike."

"And you . . .are you a warrior?"

"It is my trade," I said, "and, I suppose, my art."

She was quiet for a moment, considering. "My daughters," she said. "They would be pleased to learn from you."

"Your daughters?"

"I have no sons," she said. "Daughters only. I have seen that they are skilled in the use of the bow, and trained in other warrior's arts. To be protected by one's children, guarded by them—there is a degree of loyalty there, that one does not find in servants."

"It is an arrangement," I agreed, "that has much to be said for it."

"Much," she murmured. But it seemed that her thoughts had shifted away from military matters. And now that the music had begun again, the conversation lapsed into attentive silence. It seemed these were artists of great reputation, visitors from eastern courts.

The night drew on. When at last the time came to sleep, I was shown to a vast bed billowy with furs and goose-down pillows, in a room that smelled of flowers and cedarwood.

"Sleep well," said the servant, and in truth what with the wine and food, and our long voyage, I was half-asleep already.

I threw off my robe and sandals, and removed the gold-embroidered coverlet from the bed, drifting off in a moment or two into heavy slumber.

I woke slowly, reluctantly, to the touch of a hand upon my cheek; opened my eyes to a soft fall of dark hair and the intent regard of long-lashed eyes. The face itself was narrow and pale, almost mournful-seeming in that grey pallid light.

"Lady," I muttered, half-asleep still and gaping like a fool.

She put a finger against my lips. "Hush," she said. And I felt the warm length of her body sliding down against my own.

What happened then was sweet and inevitable, and as pleasant with a queen as with any other woman.

When I woke for the second time, she was gone. Had she not left behind a faint impression on the pillow and a lingering trace of fragrance, I might have sworn that I had dreamed that visit.

All that next day was spent in pleasant idleness, wandering through the palace grounds. At the end of one of the gardens was a long lawn where butts had been set up against the trees for target-practice. Here I found Zaidh and a dozen young maids and women, employing their bows with seasoned skill.

Today Zaidh wore a tunic, like her daughters; her long slim legs were bare. Her bow was made of some silvery-colored wood; her arrows of silver, fletched with grey gull's feathers.

The bow was long, and had a heavy draw, I thought, for a woman's weapon. Still, her aim was sure and true. I could see there was a great deal of strength in those slim arms of hers.

"Which are your daughters?" I asked her, as she stepped out of the line for a moment.

"These are all my daughters," she said.

I stared. "So many?"

She smiled, seeing my eyes fall to the slender lines of her waist and hips.

"There are twelve," she said. "The eldest has children of her own; the youngest has not yet reached womanhood. Our lives are long, and there is much leisure here. We have time for many children if it pleases us."

She said no more of my training them in warlike arts; I guessed that it had been but a pretext for conversation, and already she had forgotten it. Indeed, seeing the arrows fly true to their mark, I wondered if there was much that I could teach them.

When we met at dinner Queen Zaidh bestowed on me her grave, sweet smile, but treated me with no more intimacy than one offers any hearth-guest. Yet as darkness faded into dawn, I woke as before to see the pale circle of her face above my pillow. I wondered, after, why she chose that grey hour; maybe it was because the blood runs slowest then, and there is less will to resist.

Over breakfast the day after, Lhaera gave me a wry glance, half-mocking, half-indulgent. When three more days had gone by, that look became anxious and a little puzzled.

It was as though this country of brilliant days and soft flower-scented nights had cast a spell on me. I had meant to lie up here for a few days at most, and yet a week, two weeks slipped by without my knowing.

Cu'haid came to tell me that the ship was stocked with fresh water, dried fruit and meat, hard breads—enough to carry us for many miles along the coast. The sails were mended, the hull newly greased. I thanked him, and promised myself—and him—that we would sail on the morrow. Or maybe on the day after that.

When you have loved a woman who is without artifice, who has held out her heart to you in her two hands, you are beguiled less easily by the tremulous smile, the sidelong glance. Zaidh understood that, I think, and knew what weapons would serve her best. She was not young, and most men would have said, not beautiful. Yet she wanted me, plainly and without question, and she made herself as beautiful to me as a night full of stars. I was neither the first sailor she had lured to her bed, nor I think the last.

She called me Ezhirith, which means "Prince of the Sun," and said I had the look of a god about me. Well, as to that, I cannot say. My face has served me well enough as faces go, having a nose, two eyes, and a mouth arranged with, I suppose, some degree of symmetry. But godlike? Such words I think were but shallow flattery, more of the silken web she sought to trap me in.

The early sun streamed through the windows. Her slim white arm was thrown over me; when I went to sit up it tightened and clung.

"Zaidh," I said, rolling over on my side to look at her. Her face was soft and relaxed, a little blurred with lovemaking.

"Sweet lady," I said, "nothing would please me better, than to spend all the nights of my life in your bed. But the season is late; there is a hard sea-voyage ahead of us. We have delayed our departure long enough."

For answer she kissed me—a long slow embrace well calculated to its purpose.

"Nay, lady," I said. A sweet indolence was taking hold of me. In truth, I had nearly forgotten the purpose of our journey. I lay back and closed my eyes, surrendering to the ministrations of her lips, her clever hands.

"Dhan!" The sound of a fist pounding on the door jolted

me back to reality. I rolled out of bed and gathered up my clothes. Then I threw open the door.

Cu'haid's face was a study in embarrassment; all the same, there was a determined set to his jaw.

"The men have been waiting on the shore these two hours past," he said. "The wind and the tide are with us."

Fastening my tunic laces, I shook my head to clear the cobwebs out of it. My head felt light, my vision uncertain, as though I were half-drunk. "Tell them I'm coming," I said.

"I'll wait," Cu'haid said quietly.

Zaidh was staring furiously at him. "While I am queen in this land," she said, "I am owed some simple courtesies, I think." There was a brittle, imperious quality in her voice that was as new to me as the expression in her eyes. I wondered that she had not shown it to me before, that look of ruthlessness and raw unswerving will.

"Go," I told Cu'haid. "Make ready to sail. I will follow."

"Dhan, we are ready. It is only you who holds us back."

"Who is the master here?" asked Zaidh in a voice sharp-edged with scorn. I saw Cu'haid flush. His air of dogged patience was giving way at last to anger. I knew through the haze of wine and lust that had befogged my senses, that he had held his tongue for my sake, not wanting to shame me in Zaidh's eyes.

"Cu'haid," I said, and my tongue seemed as thick and sodden as my wits. "Forgive me, comrade, I am not myself today." Damn this long-faced witch, I thought, there was something more than wine in that flagon. Or else it is witchery that has betrayed me. I took a long slow breath, which did little to clear my head but gave me pause in which to gather my woolly thoughts.

She followed us to the palace steps; and, pale and wraithlike in her thin white gown, stood looking after us. There was something piteous about her, I thought. Her wide beseeching eyes pulled at my heart . . .

"Nay, lady," I said. I spoke the words aloud, so that Cu'haid gave me a quick look.

My mind was beginning to clear in the hot sun. "That lady has more tricks than a Ghantian warrior," I said. Cu'haid grinned, and threw an arm over my shoulders; we went down like that to the harbor, to where our shipmates waited.

The tide lifted us gently, and rocked us. There was not a breath of wind in that cloudless noon, and the men fell with a will to the oars.

"Dhan?" Her voice drifted over the white sands, sweet and dangerous as the songs of those sea-wraiths that lure men to their deaths.

Lhaera was standing in the bow, watching the shore with a look of cold fury in her eyes.

"Still she will not let you go," she said. "She has little enough pride, for a woman who calls herself a queen."

"Look," said Jhael, and I saw Zhaid's white figure moving toward the shore. She held up something that glinted silver in the sun's glare. And then we could see the graceful line of arm and shoulder as she fitted arrow to bow.

I heard the sharp intake of Lhaera's breath. "Get down," she said, and when I did not move, she jerked hard on my sleeve.

"We're out of range," I tried to say, but by that time Lhaera had me down on my knees facing her, and she was shaking her head. Her eyes had an anxious, wary look.

And then, sure-aimed and shocking in its speed over that impossible stretch of water, an arrow thudded into the hull, piercing the taut-stretched hide up close to the prow, and holding fast.

"Draw it out!" Lhaera's voice was shrill with urgency. "Draw it out and throw it into the sea."

I shook my head. "If I do that, it will rip a great hole in the hull."

"Here," Jhael said, and he handed me a knife.

I looked over the gunwale. From the shaft of the arrow,

stretching away to shore, was a silvery thread, as fine as spider's silk, barely visible against the bright glitter of the sea. As I reached out with the knife to cut through the shaft, the line pulled suddenly taut.

What happened then was a thing not to be believed, though with my own eyes I saw it. That gossamer line began to draw the ship through the water, against the current and the wind, back toward the shore, as a child might draw a toy boat on a string across a millpond.

"Cut the line," cried Lhaera. "Dhan, if you will not, give me the knife and let me do it."

Though my face still burns with dark shame at the memory, if I am to be honest I must say what I did then. Kneeling in the bow, I held fast to that ensorcelled arrow with my two hands, and defied any man, or woman either, to cut it free.

That was the first betrayal—of my purpose, my honor, of the trust my companions had placed in me. Of my manhood. It was not the last.

I remember her face, no longer sad, but with a calm, welcoming look, her pale arms reaching out to me. I remember but dimly the drugged days, the long waking nights, while my comrades waited, and paced, and cursed the summer's passing.

Lhaera came to me one day while Zaidh was away from the palace attending to affairs of state. We walked together under the oleander trees. By now the blooms had fallen; they lay scattered in pink drifts across the path.

"Listen to me, Dhan," she said, and there was both anger and pity in her eyes—pity for me, who deserved nothing but her contempt. "You know that this woman has put an enchantment on you. It is the passion she has raised up in you, that binds every one of us to her will. It is your love that draws her arrow straight and true, that gives her thin line more strength than all the power of the wind and tide." She put her hands on my shoulders, and from the fierceness of her look I thought she meant to shake me, as one shakes sense into a stubborn child. "Forswear her, Dhan. It is a false love, that comes more from witchcraft than from the heart."

I said, "The season draws on. I know you will say that is my own doing, but mightn't it be wiser now to wait for spring?"

"And will your passion be less, when you have lain in her bed for nine months more? Dhan, do you remember what Cu'haid said, when the men wanted to bide instead of leave? That we must go on, or be lost forever?" She looked at the ground, absently stirring the faded blossoms with her foot. "The men have been talking; they will not wait any longer. They say that if you will not come, then you must bide here by yourself."

"And you, Lhaera? What do you say?"

"As the men do. And Jhael and Cu'haid also."

Behind us, a woman's voice said, "You are a fool, Dhan. I knew that when first I laid eyes on you."

I turned, and looked into the cold furious eyes of the princess Razzan.

"She will not let you go," the princess said. "She will do whatever she has to do, to keep you. She recognizes no other claims, but those of her own flesh."

"What difference can it make to you, princess, whether I go or bide?"

"Indeed," she said, "you are an even greater fool than I thought. What difference, you ask?"

At that moment her face was her mother's face—leaner, harder, perhaps, but in the eyes and the set of the mouth there was that same look of ruthlessness, that was like a great wind sweeping everything before it.

She threw my words contemptuously back at me. "What difference will it make to me, when you get a child on her? What difference, when she bears a son—who by our laws must sit on the throne instead of me? According to her, I am fit only to be captain of her guard, not fit to be a queen.

Twelve daughters she has brought forth, and no male heir. But she is young yet; there is time."

I stared at her like the fool she thought I was. So after all it was not me Zaidh loved, but only the male seed I had brought to this court of women.

"Listen," said Razzan. She leaned forward and spoke rapidly into my ear. "Tonight I will slip a sleeping-draught into her wine, and I will see that the way is clear for you to escape. You must go now, tonight, for she has bewitched you; and every night you spend with her, strengthens the spell."

Yet she was cleverer than her daughter, that sad-faced queen. Somehow—though I did not see it done and could have sworn she had no hand in it—the wine-beakers were exchanged; so that it was I who drank the sleeping-draught, not Zaidh.

This time it was Razzan herself who brought my men to fetch me to the ship, and when she understood what happened, gave the order to seize me. So they dragged me naked out of those silken sheets, sullen as a thwarted child in my drugged half-sleep.

I remember, as in a fever dream, the sound of Zaidh's fury; the black fire in her eyes as she screamed out for the guard, who did not come. And then I was out of the palace, borne with the wind's speed through the stony fields, with Jhael's cloak thrown round me. I remember hanging on for dear life to a silver horn, and a silver mane, with Cu'haid, behind me, swearing and struggling to hold me upright.

I saw the sky redden with the dawn, felt the sea-wind on my face, and then my skin-boat rocking and swaying beneath me in a gentle swell.

"Drink this," Lhaera said, and she tilted some bitter-tasting potion into my mouth. After that my head cleared a little.

Zaidh came pounding down to the shore with her white

gown and her dark hair streaming, fitting her arrow as she rode.

I heard Cu'haid mutter, ''This time she shall not have us,'' and saw, through my clearing vision, that he held a knife ready in his hand.

Still her power was on me; I struggled and cursed as they held me, striving to break free.

Zaidh's arm drew back. I heard the sharp crack of the bow, and the arrow singing. The shaft came straight at our stern, that the wind and tide had turned to face the shore; it should have caught us high up, just under the gunwale.

At that instant Ghierad, who had leaped suddenly across the thwarts from amidships, threw himself on his knees into the stern. He was reaching over the side as he landed; maybe he had some mad notion of catching the arrow in his hand. In any event, his sudden weight made the stern dip a little, not much, but enough. Zaidh's arrow struck him full in the breast, and must have pierced his heart.

He coughed once, and blood welled out of his mouth. Zaidh's silken line pulled tight, and hummed with tension. It would have toppled Ghierad forward, over the stern, had not Cu'haid leaned out with his knife and cut it. Silently Jhael pulled the boy back and lowered him to the boards beside the tiller. Ghierad's eyes were wide open and staring. He had died almost at once; in that, at least, was the Sea-Mother merciful.

I felt my throat grow tight with grief and shame. To no one in particular I said, ''He need not have died. I meant to cut the line myself.''

''I know that,'' Lhaera said softly—not looking at me. ''But do you not think the gods too had a hand in this?''

She knelt beside the boy and wiped the blood from his face with a dampened cloth. They had straightened him out on his back to wait for her blessing, as priestess, before sea-burial.

''We knew from the first he was on a voyage of his own, to

some far place. Now I think he has reached his destination.''
Gently she drew down his eyelids. "Look," she said. It was
true, with his eyes closed he did not have that look of terrible
surprise that dead men so often wear; rather, there was in his
face a kind of tired acceptance, as though he had embraced
the thing he feared most in the world, and found that it held no
further terror for him.

In late summer we passed through the straits, where the
great rock looms out of the mist like a crouching beast. There
is a harbor to the west, and a steep path leading up through the
pines and olives to the Sea-Mother's temple. In that immense
echoing place carved out of living rock we gave thanks to the
Lady, as sailors have done through all the ages, for bringing
us safely to the Tideless Sea.

There are strong currents in the straits and the waters are
often choppy, though not as a rule dangerous in summer. The
weather held, though there was a hint of frost in the air,
mornings. We knew that winter was not far off when we
sailed at last into the lapis-colored waters, the white transparent sunlight of the south.

And so I end. If one day they make a hero-tale of this, it
must be in Lhaera's name, and Jhael's, and Cu'haid's, for the
truth does me little honor.

As I write this, the buds are swelling in the courtyards of
Aprilioth. The spring is lovely, in this place of fountains and
white towers. Yet when the wind blows up from the sea I feel
an old restlessness come upon me.

They say there is fighting to the east, where old King
Byzes is rattling his spears again. My sword hangs on my
chamber wall, like one of Zarimath's trophies. I see that it has
grown dull with verdigris in this island air. As soon as I have
put away my parchment, I have a mind to take it down and
polish it.

THE
FOURTH SONG

Siod'h

The sun, falling aslant through the windows, threw a circle of dusty light on Siod'h's page. He stretched, and absently rubbed the back of his neck, which had begun to ache. The last chart was finished. He blew on the ink, then rolled the sheepskin tightly and fastened it with a cord.

He got up, his chair-legs scraping loudly on the stone floor. As an afterthought he picked up the sheepskin and tucked it under his arm. Then he went out to look for Ehlreth.

He found the old man half-dozing on a bench in the west courtyard: a pleasant secluded place, warmed at this hour by the late sun. Ehlreth was leaning against the wall with his eyes closed and his face tilted to the light; the sun, westering, faintly gilded his white hair and his beard. A large grey cat, one of many that roamed the temple passages, lay with its head in the Dream-Watcher's lap.

Siod'h coughed gently. The cat, feeling Ehlreth stir, looked up at Siod'h with mild reproach.

Ehlreth's eyes opened. "Siod'h," he said, with his beautiful grave smile.

"Dream-Watcher, they sent word this morning that the boats are ready."

Clear as water those eyes were, grey as the winter sea. "And you, Siod'h? Are you ready?"

For answer Siod'h held up the sheepskin, thrusting it out before him like a talisman, or a weapon. He said, "I would have finished sooner, but I thought it best to make copies of everything. Mynach is storing them for me in the temple library. Should we fail to return . . ."

"A wise precaution," said Ehlreth. "And what have you there?"

"My route-map." Siod'h unfastened the scroll and spread it on the bench between them. The map was drawn in colored inks, with a draftsman's precise eye to detail.

"See, here are the Grey Isles, where I have marked; if we cross the channel here, and follow the mainland coast, we can beach the dugouts at the Haven; from there a track leads north to the Holy Mountains. We'll sledge the stones down to the coast by the same route. Then back by raft and boat along the coast—that will be the quickest part of the journey, but the riskiest also. While the weather holds we'll land all the stones here at the mouth of the River Hefryn, where there will be boats and men waiting."

"And then?"

"Inland by the Hefryn, the Greenwillow and its tributaries, to the Great Down."

"Here you must travel overland," Ehlreth pointed out, as he examined the map. "And again, here. A week's journey, at least."

"It will take time," Siod'h agreed, "and a great many strong backs. I left orders with Donag while I am gone to hire men from the downlands and arrange for transport—boats, sleds, whatever is necessary. Remember, the sea-voyage will be behind us. In these sheltered waterways we can work on through the autumn if we must, and into the winter."

"Aye, if you must," Ehlreth said; and it seemed to Siod'h that his eyes were troubled. "And how many have agreed to go with you to the mountains?"

"From the temple, twenty. And fivescore from the town."

"How many of those are warriors?"

"Perhaps thirty, and most of those have seen battle under Dhan." He added, "The rest know how to fight if there is need."

"Let us thank the Mother for that," said Ehlreth dryly. "Those are wild lands, betwixt the coast and the Holy Mountains."

Somewhere within the temple a bell sounded, signaling the evening meal.

"Is it as late as that?" Ehlreth murmured. As he stood he gathered up the cat, setting it gently down on the flagstones. "Come in to supper, Siod'h. We will talk while you eat."

"Dream-Watcher . . ." Siod'h took a step forward, and put out a hand as though he meant to grasp the old man's arm.

"Yes, lad?"

"I came to ask you this . . .have you looked into the crystal?"

"To see the end of your journey? Aye, lad, I have."

"Tell me what you saw."

Ehlreth shook his head. "There is nothing I can tell you, for the vision would not come clear. I could see a little way, only, and then a mist clouded my sight."

Looking into that candid, affectionate gaze, Siod'h knew that Ehlreth was hiding nothing, that he spoke only the plain truth.

"I think," Ehlreth said slowly, "it may be the power of the blue stones that obscures the vision. There exists in them an ancient and a terrible magic, in the face of which my own art is as nothing—a candle-flame against the sun.''

"Can you tell me, Ehlreth, how much time is left?''

"Who can say? A year, three years, a day? We must do what we can. Come, lad,'' he said gently. "Come to supper. There is too little meat on your bones for the task you have ahead of you. I need no magic to see that.''

Siod'h's younger sister Mara was waiting for him in Hall. She had taken of late to spending much time in the priests' house, eating meals there, joining randomly in the lessons, running errands for the novices, or simply wandering the passages without any special purpose, and certainly with no one's stated permission. The priests indulged her, clearly seeing in her a budding vocation. Siod'h said nothing, though he suspected she came there out of loneliness, or a simple need for distraction. He knew that her true interests lay elsewhere, in sword and bow and battle-strategy: in the lessons of the war-camp, for which she was still years too young.

She was sitting on the far side of the long room, her face in shadow and turned half away from him; for a curious instant he failed to recognize her.

One of the older priests—perhaps it was Ehlreth—had remarked to Siod'h that he looked at things with his nose too close to the table. It was true that Siod'h's draftsman's eye, that missed no tiniest detail, was apt sometimes to lose sight of the whole: a well-loved face becoming a series of planes and angles, a pleasing architecture of flesh and bone. Now for once he stood back, as it were, and saw his sister's face as another man might see it. He realized with a shock that the wide mouth, the round childish cheeks, the scholar's brow—features that until now had seemed vaguely at odds with one another—had somehow reassembled themselves, had fallen into harmony, had acquired, in fact, a stern but unmistakable beauty.

At this moment, as he sat down across from her, the mouth and jaw were formidable.

"I'm coming with you," she advised Siod'h—as usual, without preamble.

"Child, you are not, this is no kind of journey for a maid."

"Arun is going, and I'm twice—three times—the warrior he is. You should remember, it was you who said so."

His mouth quirked. "That may be, but you must allow he has attained manhood, and can therefore make his own choices."

"And I being a child must do whatever I am bade." Her grey eyes shot fire at him. "Dhan wanted our cousin Thieras to go with him."

"But she did not," Siod'h pointed out, as gently as he could.

"Why not? I should have, in an instant, if he had asked me."

"You must ask Thieras that question." But he saw that she must have an answer from him, and he sighed. "I think," he said, "that she saw what must be the true order of things."

He took up one of her thin brown hands—awkwardly, not knowing quite what to do with it. He squeezed it in comradely fashion, and let it drop.

"And how can you know it is in the order of things, that I should be left behind?"

"Only the Dream-Master can know that. I can only say that it will be a hard and dangerous journey. We will not finish the task this summer; in truth we may not finish it before the end comes. And who knows when that will be? By then you may be a woman grown, and a warrior—if indeed that is what your mind is set on."

"And if the end comes not late, but soon?"

She spoke of it matter-of-factly, as he did. There were some, older than she, who would not have used those words; who could not mention, without flinching, the shadow that hung over them.

"Then you will go with the others to the high lands, out of

the sea's reach. They will be needing warriors there, even such young warriors as you . . .''

She feigned petulance, but it did not sit well on her; her mouth was too honest for such tricks. And then, as though glimpsing herself in his eyes, she grinned.

"Well, anyway," she conceded, "I know how slow you are, with your finicking priest's ways. You will be years getting there, and more years getting back. As for me, I shall spend the time in sword-practice. I know you will think better of your foolishness, soon enough, and send for me."

They left in early morning from the West Harbor. Crowds lined the quay and the wet rocky shore; flocks of children, hoping for a bird's-eye view, raced madly up and down the cliff-paths.

It was high summer, a day of clear skies and glittering water. Above the town the long fields were bright with vetch and meadowsweet. Vivid patches of goldenrod streaked the hills like paint. The women, especially, had tried to make the day seem festive: turning out in their most colorful garments, with scarves and handkerchiefs fluttering. Yet the faces on the shore, seen close to, looked drawn and anxious. What hung in the air that morning was neither excitement nor celebration, but a tired stubborn rejection of despair.

Arms waved, voices called out to them. Mara, wearing an old grey tunic and a look of purest pathos, threw them a warrior's salute, and stalked away. As they rowed out of the harbor they could see the other women, like flowers in their windblown finery, still waving from the water's edge.

They circled the Grey Isles, westward, then rowed north with the tide, toward the mainland coast. The prevailing winds were against them, but for the present these were no more than light airs. On the return voyage, when they most needed its help, they would have the wind at their backs.

As they rested for a while in a stretch of quiet water, the

priest Esghar leaned forward and tapped Siod'h's shoulder.
He gestured to the red-haired lad behind him.

"Let us change places," Esghar said. "Young Bryn
here, he spends all his time thinking up questions for which I
have no answers. You are the geomancer, you talk to him."

Siod'h took Esghar's place next to the red-haired
townsman. He had spoken to Bryn before, and had been
struck by the quickness of his mind. The lad might have made
a priest, had he not been so eager for a warrior's life.

"Well, Bryn?" he said. "Esghar tells me you have picked
his brain clean, and are not yet content."

The boy grinned. He had a pleasant open face, sunburned
and heavily freckled. His green eyes were intelligent and
good-humored.

"If you want to catch trout you should follow the river
upstream, my old granny always said." He gulped water
from his goatskin and wiped his mouth with the back of his
hand. "Listen," he went on, "I know a soldier marches
where he's told to march, without asking questions. And so
when Dhan said, 'My kinsman Siod'h needs thirty good men
for a dangerous mission—and no reasons given—I held up
my sword with the rest of them."

"And grateful I am for that," Siod'h remarked. "Had
Dhan told you what the mission was, you might have been in
no hurry to step forward."

"Be that as it may, I know now. But I've been puzzling my
head over the reasons. We are to fetch these rocks from over
there "—with his right arm he made a sweeping gesture to the
northwest, conjuring up vast distances—"and haul them all
the way to *there* . . ." Another expansive gesture, eastward.

Siod'h nodded.

"Well, with due respect, and speaking as one who has
always looked for the fastest and easiest way . . .surely, in
those northern mountains, so far out of the sea's reach

. . .Sir, had you never thought of building your circle where the stones already are?''

Siod'h smiled. ''A tempting thought,'' he said. ''But no, there is some method in my seeming madness.'' He was disconcerted for a moment, realizing that he had nothing on which to write. He began, with one finger held up, to trace in the air long lines radiating outward from a central point.

''We must abide by the natural order, by the pattern of things. Here is the site of the old temple, on the high downs where the straight roads cross, where all things come together. Here, always, since the beginning of the world, has power flowed inward. Here must the great circle be built.'' He glanced into Bryn's intent young face. ''And here are the stones of ancient power. Our task is to bring the one to the other.''

Along the mainland coast huge promontories of grey rock rose sheer and forbidding against the sky. Here the great rollers pounded in from the open sea, to smash beneath the cliffs, their white advancing lines as straight as the ones on Siod'h's charts.

Everywhere along this wild shore were hidden rocks and treacherous cross-currents that spelled disaster for the unwary. It was a coast that had claimed more than its fair share of lives. It was said the folk that lived above the cliffs need cut no trees for firewood; they had only to visit the lonely beaches at low tide after a storm, and gather up the splintered wreckage of boats.

As they rowed westward toward the Haven, the cliff-faces were broken by many small half-hidden coves, and sometimes the broad sweep of a sandy beach. Thousands of sea-birds—cormorants, guillemots, kittiwakes—nested in the rocks above these tideswept bays.

The current was stronger now; rowing against it, they soon felt the strain in their backs and arms. The boy Arun already looked close to exhaustion. He was no more than sixteen, a

slight dark-haired lad with dreaming eyes and a smile of
sudden intense sweetness. Orphaned at birth, he had been
raised as Bryn's hearth-brother, and at manhood the two had
sworn comradeship in blood. Arun's skill was with the
harp—he had little talent for weapons; but he would not be
separated from his friend.

"Rest awhile, lad," said the townsman Griffid. He was a
huge man, as strong as an ox, but kind-hearted for all that.
"You too, Ewain. Cay and I will take up the slack. Young
Arun, you give us a song."

Arun needed no urging. He carried his harp with him
everywhere, wrapped in a piece of doeskin against the damp.
Shipping his oars, he took up the instrument and set it against
his shoulder. Underneath his hands the sweet notes rushed
out like water.

To begin, he played the Tale of Gubwin's Daughter—a
rollicking, slightly bawdy air that brought grins to his listen-
ers' faces. He went on in that vein for a while, improvising
and embroidering love-lays, dance-tunes, tales of ancient
heroes. But then the mood and the tempo of his music altered,
and there swelled from his harpstrings a slow, lovely air of
antique days. If it had a name once, or words, they were long
since forgotten; all that remained was that sweet, strange,
throat-catching melody. It was the music of autumn, a lament
for the doomed year, when spring is too far away for hope,
and beauty too much for the heart to bear.

Arun put up a hand to push back the hair that had fallen
across his face, and briefly, his eyes met Siod'h's. They were
strange eyes—a very pale clear violet, startling in his sun-
browned face. Fringed with dark lashes, they were innocent
as a fawn's; and like a fawn's, there was something in them
unreachable, unhuman.

The music rippled gently into silence. Siod'd felt a long
slow shiver run down his spine. That, he thought, is a song
for the world's ending. For a long time no one spoke; and

when they did, it was to talk of ordinary things. That day, they asked for no more harp-songs.

The sun reached the mid-heavens and began its slow descent. An hour or so past noon the weather changed abruptly. Grey clouds moved across the sun, and the wind freshened. Without warning they were caught up in strong headwinds and heavy seas.

The dugout was solid and broad-beamed, near impossible to capsize, but by the same token, clumsy; and for men used to the agile response of a skin-boat, difficult to maneuver in these treacherous seas. The wind blew salt spray into their teeth; immense white-crested hills of water marched toward them. They cursed, and bent their backs to the oars, feeling the despair that comes in the grip of the sea's raw, mindless strength.

Suddenly a violent gust of wind caught the bow and slapped it sideways. Across that grey tumbled waste a monstrous wave hurled itself upon them, striking them squarely broadside. It lifted their heavy boat like a chip of wood and flung it shoreward, straight toward the foaming rocks.

They had lost sight of the other boats; they were entirely cut off, alone. Had they called out for help none could have heard, or helped them, in those howling seas.

Siod'h felt the dugout shudder and groan beneath him; there was a sudden sickening plunge, a terrible sound of wood splintering. He dragged in a great chestful of air, and then the waves crashed over him; he felt himself dragged, lifted, spun end over end like a brine-soaked log, and finally, unexpectedly, disgorged.

After a time he was dimly conscious of sand and pebbles under his palms and against his cheek. Without moving his head he coughed up a stomachful of salt water. Only then did he lift his chin, painfully, and open his eyes.

He was lying on a wide stretch of wet sand. The sea, purely on whim, he imagined, had tossed him clean over and beyond the rocks. He rolled over and dragged his wet hair out of his eyes. He thought at first the beach was entirely empty; then, a little distance off, he saw a solitary shape lying motionless, face upward.

"Bryn." He sobbed out the name as he ran. He turned the boy over, so that the seawater could run out of his mouth, and let out his own breath in a great sigh when he heard Bryn groan, and cough.

Bryn staggered as he got to his feet; Siod'h put an arm across his shoulders to support him. The townsman was twisting his head first one way and then the other, in a kind of frenzy, as his eyes searched the empty shore.

Siod'h shook his head. Bryn stared at him, wild-eyed. "All?"

Siod'h said dully, "I have looked. They are not here. The sea must have taken them."

He waited until he saw that first shock of loss subside into a kind of dazed calm. Then he took Bryn's arm and led him up the pale sloping sands toward the cliffs.

From the shingle, a narrow path wound its way up the face of the sea-cliff. Gulls and cormorants screamed down at them as they climbed. The wind had died, but a thin drenching rain continued to fall.

They reached the top of the cliff and came out upon a gorse-grown moor, bare but for a few gaunt thorn-trees, spectral in the mist. Both of them by now were shivering violently from cold and shock. Their sodden garments hung upon them, dank as seaweed.

Presently they came upon a huddle of outbuildings and then a turf hut, heather-thatched. The hut seemed long un-used, the air damp and musty-smelling, but the thatch was intact still, and kept out the rain. At that moment the place looked as welcoming to Siod'h and Bryn as any palace.

A few scraps of kindling wood and some larger branches were scattered by the hearth. Siod'h found his flint and skystone; before long they had a fire going, and stripping off their drenched tunics, they hung them up to dry.

Bryn went on shivering for some time; his arms and back were covered with gooseflesh.

"Here," said Siod'h, "I'll share these with you." He had found, tossed into a corner, a rank-smelling heap of skins.

"Well," said Siod'h. Although hungry, he was warm and moderately comfortable. Already his thoughts were turning to practical matters.

"It may be that we are misplaced, but we are not lost, entirely. So often have I charted this country, that it is all writ plain in my head. We have only to follow the sun when it shows its face again, and we must come to the Haven, or else the waters that flow into it."

He glanced at Bryn, and was worried by what he saw. By now the fire should have warmed the lad; yet still he wore that dazed and wretched look, and could not leave off shuddering. Perhaps it was shock, or a deeper grief than Siod'h had guessed at. Or else the boy had taken a hard chill that was turning to fever.

"Go to sleep," Siod'h told him. "I will keep the fire going, so that our clothes dry. Tomorrow I will try to remember what I know of rabbit-snaring, that my cousin Thieras taught me."

There was no answer. The boy huddled deeper in his musty skins. Finally he said, in an anguished voice, "Siod'h, he is lost and afraid, and calling out to me."

"Who, then?" Siod'h knew the answer well enough, yet he was loath to hear the name spoken.

"He whom the sea has taken. We are not so easily parted, we two who are brothers in blood."

"Sleep," said Siod'h. Though he knew they sprang out of a sick fancy, a fever-dream, still such words, spoken in this lonely place, made the hair stir on his nape.

Indeed, when night came, he could have sworn he heard,

somewhere in the great dark beyond their walls, a thin sound like a child wailing. It was an owl, he told himself, or a night-jar—anyway, no human voice.

But in the night there was a soft and diffident knocking, that at first Siod'h thought must be a bit of loose thatch blowing in the wind. Then he heard his own name, and Bryn's, spoken; and looking up from the fire, he felt something ice-cold run down his spine.

Arun stood just inside the doorway, the mist curling in behind him. Rain clung in beads to his dark hair, catching the firelight and glittering like gems. He smiled, with a curious shy hesitation, as though uncertain of his welcome. When he spoke, it was to Bryn.

"Brother," he said, "did you believe me drowned, and grieve for me? You know I have as many lives as a mountain cat."

Bryn's broad face shone with a fierce unquestioning joy. Long after the pair had fallen asleep, Siod'h watched, and wondered, and fed the fire.

Arun's cheek, smooth-fleshed and fine-boned as a maid's, lay close to Bryn's; their faces in sleep were as innocent as children's. Yet through all that long night was Siod'h wakeful and uneasy, listening to the rain dripping down the eaves, and the soft soughing of the wind among the thorns. He was haunted by a vague apprehension of disorder, a sense that the pattern of things, somewhere, somehow, had been twisted subtly awry.

Siod'h woke to the warmth of the early sun upon his face. He yawned and stretched, and went out to look for water.

Their hut stood in a high windy meadow, bordered with rowans and hawthorns in summer bloom. A straight track, deep-worn by long use, led off to the northwest.

"Did I not tell you," said Siod'h, "this country is well-traveled," and they set out in the mild morning, gathering handfuls of blackberries as they went.

Presently the open moorland gave way to bramble thickets and thinly scattered oakwoods. Kingfishers flashed among the sunlit leaves; beneath the trees were bright clumps of bluebells and anemones. The dappled shade made a pleasant respite from the midday heat.

As they went on, however, the track grew narrow and twisting, choked with undergrowth. The trees crowded closer, shutting out the sun. Their gnarled trunks were grey with lichen, their branches half-smothered in vines and mistletoe. There were no bluebells here, only those pale blooms, like the ghosts of flowers, that spring up in dark places under the moldering leaves. No birds sang in the grey-green twilight; the thick moss hushed even the sound of footsteps.

Behind him, Siod'h heard Arun cry out in a queer choked voice, and when he turned he saw that the boy's face had gone a sickly white.

"We are lost, Siod'h. This place has a spell upon it, and now that we are in, we will never find our way out again." Arun was whispering, as though he feared to disturb the heavy silence.

"Don't be a fool," Siod'h said, more sharply than he had intended. "The track is plain before us—we have only to follow it. What kind of a path goes into a forest and does not come out again?"

The words were lightly spoken, yet no sooner were they out of his mouth, than he would have swallowed them. The look of naked terror on the boy's face brought a chill to his own breast, for he could see writ plain there, the answer to his question.

To one of Siod'h's training, the use of magic was no different in kind from the pharmacist's lore, the skill of the astronomer or the mathematician. One learned the rules, the formulae—one came to understand the intricate and delicate, yet generally predictable pattern of things. And having accomplished that—having mastered one's tools like any good craftsman—one achieved a degree of control.

But then for a second or two he looked into the purple wells of Arun's eyes, and saw reflected there a thing outside all sense, all order: that other, darker and more ancient magic, that serves the Lords of Chaos.

Siod'h shook his head as though to clear it of nightmares.

"Look there," Bryn whispered. Vague and ghostlike in the gloom, a young roe deer had emerged from a thicket. Scenting man, she paused and her head went up, but she stood her ground, her brown gaze meeting theirs with a disquieting boldness.

Had she spoken aloud, in the language of man, the warning could have been no plainer. "Turn back," her eyes pleaded. Delicately, anxiously, her small forefeet scraped the mossy ground. And then she tossed her head and danced away into the shadows. She looked back over her shoulder as she went, as much as to say, "Come. Follow."

Darkness was gathering, and a cold mist was rising from the ground. As it coiled round their hips their teeth began to chatter, and painful shudders racked their bodies. This chill that had crept upon them out of a summer's noon was more fierce than the cold of deepest winter—a cold such as the priests said would come at the world's end, when all warmth, all light rushed outward like the tide, to be lost in the great dark between the stars.

In the center of the mist was a great squat thing, humped, hunched, gigantic. It was a creature born of night and chaos; a core of utter blackness with edges that seemed indefinite, uncertain, flowing out into the grey dim air as black dye diffuses into water.

As they stared the shape grew larger, taller, as though it were feeding upon the shadows of the forest, gathering darkness and immensity until it loomed above them, blotting out the trees and sky.

Arun had pressed as close as he could to Bryn for warmth, or comfort. Bryn, his ruddy face gone the color of chalk, was clutching a thick branch he had snatched up from the ground.

Siod'h stared, with his head tilted back, in fascinated horror. Above that mounded blackness was there, surely, the semblance, the suggestion of a face?

Gradually it took shape and substance—the massive and misshapen brow, with the darkness streaming away from it like tangled hair; the outline of the cheek, the jaw, and a single round patch of lesser darkness that, growing plainer, took on the appearance of an eye.

The eye was closed; the grey-black lid lay across it like a shutter. Beneath the lid a thin line of reddish light gleamed, and as they watched that line began to widen.

Of their own accord, they could no more have torn their eyes away, than a rabbit can stir from the iron grip of the ferret's gaze. But at that instant, as the great eye began to open, there was a faint rustling and pattering in the underbrush—a sound as slight as the wind makes among the branches. And then with the wind's swiftness, there burst from among the black columns of the trees a herd of fallow deer. Flank to flank, shoulder to shoulder they ran, their pale hides gleaming in the dusk, not timidly, as is the nature of deer, but in heedless, headlong flight, like cattle.

The monstrous head turned, as the stone face of a hill might turn, and the eye, half-open now and burning with a red, baleful light, turned with it. The deer rushed on, the white flags of their tails vanishing into darkness, and the eye followed them.

Then sudden as lightning a raven dropped from the darkening air; another followed, and another, until the forest was filled with their harsh cries and the thunder of their black wings.

In one swift and deadly motion a beak pierced the eye, below the lid. Again and again the birds struck, circling and climbing into the black branches, and returning to strike again. Out of the ruins of the eye there gouted forth blackness; the great head rolled and twisted in agony, the tendrils of hair writhing out on the grey air like snakes. Slowly the head collapsed into the mountainous shoulders, and those in turn fell in upon themselves, diminished, like a punctured bladder. The creature's life, the very stuff of its being, was gushing out of the wounded eye, was flowing away like black water across the ground.

Afterward there was an immense silence, which filled slowly with the sounds of birds and the small ordinary noises of the wood. The summer's warmth crept back into the forest, into their chilled bones; yet it brought with it little strength or courage.

Siod'h looked into the blanched faces of his companions. The thing, whatever it was, was destroyed, defeated; the way lay open to them. Yet was their will sapped, their resolve weakened; they hung back in terror of what might lie ahead.

There sprang to Siod'h's mind the heroes of the old songs, who, having conquered some fearsome obstacle, encountered ever greater and more terrible tests. Suppose this monstrous thing were a harbinger, only, and all the dreadful ranks of Chaos followed after?

"You would do well to come out of that place," said a female voice. Though light and young, it was the voice of one who knows her own mind, and means to be obeyed.

A young woman stepped unexpectedly out of the deep shade. There was a bow on her back, a spear in her right hand. Beyond, Siod'h could sense rather than see a dozen others, their slim shapes half-hidden among the foliage.

"Come out into the sunlight," the woman said. "It is safer there, where the light drives out the shadows."

She led the three of them, as one might lead lost children, into an open glade where grey rocks stood up among bracken and long grass. Here, under scattered larch and alder trees, grew foxglove and yellow summer lilies.

Siod'h looked with undisguised curiosity at the warrior-woman. She was tall for a woman, with a long-limbed, smoothly muscled body, and the strong arms and shoulders of an archer. She put him in mind a little of his kinswoman Thieras—though his cousin was dark, and this woman fair as sunlight. Her face was broad, high-cheekboned, the mouth wide, the nose short and generously freckled; a rather ordinary pleasant face made remarkable by a pair of hyacinth-colored, curiously upward-slanting eyes.

"I am Ryll," she said, "princess of the tribe of Grymarch." And gesturing: "These are my maidens." Sunburnt though her face and arms were, where her tunic sleeve fell back her skin showed white as milk.

"This wood has an evil reputation," she said. "You would have done well to take the long way round it."

Feeling obscurely that he must defend himself, Siod'h said, "There was a straight track, and we followed it."

She gave him a small, and he fancied cryptic, smile. It seemed to him that this woman thought a great deal more than she said. "You are not the first to set out on a straight track and find it leads to places you would prefer not to have gone. Anyway, in this country things are often not what they seem. After a while you learn to be wary, and maybe a little devious. But," she said, "you have not told me—or maybe I have not asked you—your destination."

"North," Siod'h said. "To the mountain of the blue stones."

He could see she knew the place he meant. She waited for him to go on, but he had already had one lesson in caution. "I am a priest," he told her. "It is one of our holy places." For the present, he decided, that was explanation enough.

"We are well-met," she said, "for it happens my mother's village lies to the north of here, and we are traveling the same road. We are ordinary folk, not holy people," she added, "but unless you would rather travel alone . . ."

There was, in her voice and her manner, no hint of mockery, only an easy good-humor.

"We would be honored by your company," Siod'h said, and meant it. In truth, he felt that without companionship their spirits might fail them altogether.

As night drew in they camped in another open, grassy place, and built a great fire to drive the shadows back. Ryll's women had been foraging as they marched; before long there rose a savory smell of roast rabbit and herbs.

When they had eaten, Arun, who was restless without an instrument in his hands, borrowed a stringbox from one of the women. He played a quick run or two, experimenting; then a suite of dances, drawing from the coarse strings an astonishing richness. Gradually, as he played, his face took on a rapt and distant look; the music changed, slowed, became remote and dreamlike. His fingers searched out the notes with a kind of puzzlement, as though rediscovering some half-forgotten melody.

Hearing that music Ryll's maidens stirred uncomfortably, and whispered amongst themselves.

Arun began to sing then, in his sweet high voice.

> "Vivid in color is that land as a wild bird's egg.
> Golden the leaves of the oak in every season.
> In that bright wood, under the shining branches
> the faces of the people are beautiful as flowers.
> Immortal are they, and without flaw."

Arun was lost in the dim corridors of his music. He did not seem to notice that Ryll's maidens had drawn away to the far side of the fire, as though he had become in some way unclean, or tainted by disease.

Bryn saw, and his color rose. He crouched at Arun's side, and put his hand on his friend's shoulder as though to comfort or reassure him. And he stared across the fire at Ryll with an angry question in his eyes.

"Yes," Ryll murmured; only Siod'h was close enough to catch those whispered words. "If they could, they would put more than a fire betwixt themselves and the boy."

"Why do they treat him so? What offense has he given? He is a gentle lad, and means harm to no one."

Ryll said sharply, "What is it they teach you, in that priest-house? Use your eyes, Siod'h. And if your eyes tell you nothing—then use what other senses you have. Look at him—quick now, while the fire is low, and the dark is behind him."

Siod'h looked then, and saw for himself. Arun had finished his song; now he sat hunched and silent, his chin resting in his hands as he stared into the glowing embers. Around him, faint and wavering, but unmistakable in the darkness, there clung a pale cool luminescence, like moon-light glowing from within the flesh.

"You see," said Ryll. Her voice, usually so brusque, had the sad and gentle certainty of a doctor who, discovering a sickness or a great wound, pronounces it beyond the hope of cure.

"He is no longer one of us, Siod'h. No longer mortal. He has been with the faerie kind, and they have claimed him for their own. As long as he is among us, none of us is safe; for, innocent as he may be, he is like a beacon burning in the night, leading the powers of darkness to us."

He stared at her, feeling, with the sharpness of a spear-thrust, the truth behind her words.

"As a rule," said Ryll, "the dark lords are not much concerned with ordinary folk, and will leave us to go about our business. It is when those others, those dwellers in the Bright Worlds, descend into our world, that the darkness follows after. Thus does one great army march forth to meet another, and that ancient war, that has been waged since the first days, comes to be fought here, on our own ground. Willy-nilly we are caught up in it, and no man, or woman, can stand apart. For better or worse, we must choose one side or the other."

Siod'h said, "Lady, you speak of ordinary folk. Yet I have seen your eyes look out to me from the face of the roe deer, and the raven."

"I have some small arts, to be sure. Who could survive in

these ensorcelled lands, without some knowledge of magic? But I am mortal, my women are mortal. If we are wounded, in our own shapes or any other, we bleed, and we die. That boy there—if you struck him down with your sword, do you think you could harm him? At worst he might vanish before your eyes. He belongs to the People of the Light. Their wounds do not bleed as ours do."

"Well," she said, and gathering her cloak about her, she rolled abruptly away from him, turning her face toward the fire. "Now I have said more than I meant to say, and it is time to sleep."

She did not stir again that night, or speak; and Siod'h lay awake for a long time, listening to her slow soft breath mingled with the sound of the nightwind, and the faint wordless melody the sentry hummed to keep herself awake.

In the morning they set out over the high moors. A bleak lonely country this, where the wind moaned incessantly among the thorns, and the grey bones of the land thrust up through the heather and coarse tawny grass. But here in the open, where few shadows were, with the sun of late summer warming the mild wet air and the track running straight and even over the ground, it was possible to believe there was order and symmetry in the world.

Toward nightfall they came over a rise of land and saw, among scattered stands of mountain ash, a circle of watch-fires burning. As they drew closer they could hear voices, the sound of reed-pipes, a snatch of bawdy song.

"At Creagh's Court," sang a loud, cheerful, untrained voice, "I took my choice of wine and mead, of blue-eyed maid and black-haired wench . . ."

"I know that voice," cried Siod'h. "Mother of us all, I know that voice."

Shouting and waving his arms like one demented, he raced off through the twilight. "Ynas!" he called out as he ran. "Ynas!"

Wonderingly, half-disbelieving, the reply came: "Siod'h? Are you not drowned, then?"

All Siod'h's shyness, his scholarly reserve fell away like a cast-off garment, as he grasped Ynas the boat-builder by both his brawny arms. A hundred others—his whole lost company—crowded round them, shouting questions.

Winded by his run, and laughing besides, Siod'h managed to gasp out, "No, you great fool, I am alive, as you can well see. And Bryn too, and Arun."

Then sobering as cold water came sudden remembrance, and his smile faded. "But Griffid is lost, and Esghar, and Cay and Ewain—all those who were with us."

Hearing that, they fell silent; for there was no man among them had not lost a friend in that wreck, or a kinsman.

After a time someone said, "And these maidens?" For by now Ryll and her women had caught up and stood waiting, amiably enough, outside the circle.

Siod'h said, "Let me present to you the Princess Ryll, of the tribe of Grymarch, and her warriors. We owe our lives to these maidens, for they found us in danger and brought us safe out of it."

"Trust a scholar," said Bryn, "to strip a good tale down to the dry bones. Give us something to wet our throats, and a place by the fire, and Arun and I will give you the meat and juice of that story."

But in fact it was left to Bryn to tell what had befallen them. Arun sat in abstracted silence, offering nothing, not so much as a ripple of the strings to underscore Bryn's narrative, scarcely seeming even to listen.

As it happened, Bryn had a gift for storytelling. So vivid was his account of their journey through the dark wood, and their meeting with the shadow-demon, that hearing it retold Siod'h felt the hair stir on his neck.

It was full dark when the tale was finished. They yawned and stretched, threw logs on the fires, and rolled themselves into their cloaks; though more than one man, before he slept, peered nervously into the shadows.

Ryll made her bed a litttle distance off, with her maidens beyond her. Observing the grace and precision of her movements as she spread and smoothed her cloak and laid her weapons—spear, bow, quiver—near to hand, Siod'h felt for her a rush of comradeship and pure affection. Here, he thought, was one who like himself loved order—for its power against chaos, and for its own sake.

She must have felt his eyes on her, for she turned and for a moment their glances met, and held. He saw her hand move a little, as though she meant to reach out to him. Then a branch crackled, exploding into flame; she started and looked away.

The morning was overcast, and smelled of autumn. They passed through a narrow valley with a stream running through it; mist-shrouded trees sprang wraithlike out of the steep bracken-covered hillsides.

The land rose gradually into brown and purple uplands. Here the gorse and heather grew sparsely on the hard ground, among jagged outcroppings of grey rock. From time to time they crossed other tracks leading off to the east and west. Whenever they approached one of these crossroads Siod'h half-expected Ryll to take her leave. As the morning wore on, he was both pleased and puzzled to find that her little band of women continued to march behind him.

He was not one to let a riddle hang in the air, and he said to her, finally, "Your mother's village . . .surely it cannot be much farther now?"

She looked at him with surprise. "Did you not know? We passed by the crossroads two hours since." She laughed, a sound pleasant as birdsong on the grey air. "Are you so weary of our company, then?"

"On the contrary, I am delighted with it."

"I could have marched them all home," she said by way of explanation. "But it is the easiest time of year, between midsummer and harvest-rites. The evenings are long, the nights are warm—and the young men have too much time on their hands." Her shrug was eloquent. "Besides, I have a great curiosity to see this holy place of yours."

The road led upward, straight and uninterrupted, to the northeast. On every side was the same wide bleak vista of heather and bog and broken stone. Above and beyond, like a blue shadow across the land, lay the ancient hills.

They climbed higher. Now, in the distance, where the land fell away to the north, they could see the glint of open water, smooth and dull as pewter.

By noon they had neared the summit. Exposed in winter to the full fury of wind and rain, this was even now in high summer a raw desolate place. Today the air was grey and curiously still; they could hear no sound anywhere—neither the movement of the wind in the bent and stunted trees, nor the voices of birds, nor any of the small stirrings and scurryings that break the huge silence of the moors.

Their own voices had died away to whispers. Puzzled and uncertain, they paused in that breathless quiet, listening to their hearts beating in their throats.

Then Siod'h cried out suddenly, "I see them!" His voice shook with excitement. "Bryn, Ynas, come quickly, we have found the place."

With those words the spell was broken, and they followed Siod'h up over the last ridge beneath the summit.

"Look there," said Siod'h. His voice was steadier now, his eyes rapt as a child's. "They are as Ehlreth described them. The blue stones, whose roots go to the belly of the world."

All along the mountain's southern crest were jagged outcroppings of green and grey-blue rock. Huge slabs and columns of this stone, pried loose by centuries of hard frosts, had toppled and crashed down upon the slopes below. There—immense, smooth-sided, darkly polished in the damp air—they lay scattered like slain giants upon the scree.

Calm though the day was, the air seemed charged, vibrant. If one looked in a certain way, one could almost imagine that the ground shimmered, as in fierce summer heat.

Ryll's women stirred uneasily, their eyes grown suddenly huge. They looked half-ready to fight, or run, their lean bodies arched with tension. Ryll's knuckles showed white as she tightened her grip upon her spear.

"Softly," Siod'h told her. "There is no danger." But in truth he was as frightened as she. The priests had spoken of charmed ground, of rock-magic, of the ancient power that flowed from the mountain's roots. But nothing had prepared him for this blind elemental force that leaped out at him, palpable and shocking as a blow to the face.

"Such power," Ryll whispered. "This is the oldest magic, the earth-magic. If you tamper with this, Siod'h, it will destroy you."

"Power can be tamed," he said. "Wind, water, fire—we have turned them all to our purposes."

"Not this," Ryll said. "This is indifferent to man. It serves only itself."

For answer, Siod'h took her by the arm and led her across the rough ground, to where one of the smooth dark stones lay half-buried in scree.

"In the temple," he said. "They teach us the Law of Congruity, which says that force must be bound with like force, by the thing that shares its nature. Thus the trees that, bending, break the wind's power; the wall of fire around the burning wood; the oil poured upon the wild sea. So the gods of underearth must be bound by the force that lives within the deep places, inside the rock."

He knelt, and put both his hands upon the stone. It was perhaps the bravest thing he had ever done. Seeing his intention, Ryll's eyes widened and her face turned chalk-white. But all Siod'h felt, touching the stone, was a vague tingling that ran up his forearms, no more than the sensation one sometimes gets from touching metal on a clear day in winter.

"You see," he said. He stood up. "It is a question of

patterns. No weaker force will bind the old gods, the faceless ones. Not wind, not fire, or water. Only this.''

Long before committing himself to this journey Siod'h had, in his usual painstaking fashion, drawn up his plans; now, taking one step at a time, he set about their execution. He called into council all those men who had priest's training, and invited the Princess Ryll to join them.

''Before the stones can be moved,'' he said, ''we must build sleds, and for that we will need oak-timber.''

Ynas turned and let his gaze wander down the bare stony hillside. ''You won't find it here,'' he said with sour amusement.

Siod'h's smile was a little sheepish. ''Route-maps are one thing,'' he admitted, ''but until you can chart the terrain for yourself . . .''

''A day's journey to the east,'' said Ryll, interrupting, ''there is an oak-forest, very old and very large, with more wood than you could possibly find a use for. Feanna!''

One of her women stepped forward—a big-boned lass of seventeen with large competent hands and a pleasant air of nonchalance.

''For now,'' Ryll told her, ''you are captain of woodcutters. You are to take six of the women with you to the Great Forest—any six you choose. Siod'h will tell you what you are to do there.''

Siod'h sent her a look of gratitude, which she acknowledged with a gently mocking grin. He gave the woman Feanna instructions for the cutting of the oak-timbers, and put most of his men into her charge, keeping back only those who were skilled in rock-patterning. With those few, he would begin the tasks of measuring, matching, choosing, and plotting the removal of the stones.

The weather had turned unseasonably cool, and a chill wind blew steadily across the unprotected slopes. Measuring lines and marking stones slipped out of hands grown stiff and clumsy with the cold. Too, there was something in this charged air that sapped the strength, making a morning's work seem as long and as tiring as a three-days' labor.

The adept Maen, on whom Siod'h had counted for his quick mind and his knowledge of rock-magic, was utterly unnerved whenever he came near the stones. Those massive presences, featureless and yet curiously watchful, the witch-light that in darkness flickered over them like summer lightning, the sense of brooding and oppressive power—these things inspired in Maen a deep and superstitious terror. In the end Siod'h sent him back to the camp, where Ryll's women set him to work plaiting strips of hide for rope.

Oddly, the boy Arun seemed to thrive while others grew anxious and exhausted. Color had returned to his wan cheeks; he seemed to draw from this place a new strength, a vivid energy.

At night they huddled around the fires, and each night Arun sang to his borrowed stringbox, his clear young voice rising above the wind's incessant whine. And though the women would not come near, still they listened, and smiled and wept in spite of themselves, for no one of ordinary feeling could hear those songs and be unmoved.

Siod'h had devised a system of pulleys and levers by which he meant, once the timber arrived, to hoist the stones onto the sleds. When he began to experiment with it, he found the stones far heavier and more awkward than he had calculated. It seemed, indeed, as though the stones had roots that clung to the very heart of underearth; and he sought through his memory for some spell, some formula that might discharge this relentless flow of power inward, downward, into the mountain's core.

The days ran together, became a week. Siod'h realized now that he had underestimated the time needed to load the stones and to transport them, and besides that, the timber-cutters had not yet returned.

He could feel a kind of sick apathy growing in him, breeding self-doubt and deadening his resolve. It was an old, familiar companion, this black mood, and he knew that once it gained a firm hold on him, it could be days or weeks before it lifted. It was to Ryll that he turned finally: more and more he had come to depend on that resourceful intelligence of hers, that wise, cheerful self-assurance.

He said, "I was foolish, thinking I could accomplish this thing alone. I have too few men, there is too little left of the summer. I need tribes, armies . . . find them for me, Ryll, and I will pay you as much as you wish, in silver."

She laughed. "I'll take your silver, though the Mother knows where I'll spend it. But listen," she said, and her eyes lit up, as they did when one of her ideas came to her. "You can pay me in better coin than that. Teach me your skill, the builder's art. I am tired of living like a wild deer in the forest. I went to a city once. Or maybe a village, you would call it. But it had roads leading up to it, a wall of stones around it, and within were shops and market squares, and great houses the size of twenty huts. I would build a city like that. I would live in a great house with oaken walls, and a door of hammered bronze. And I would have smooth sheets to my bed, like the city women have." She gave him a sly look. "I liked the shops. Maybe I will go there again, and spend your silver. But teach me to build a town, and I will call up all my mother's tribes, and my mother's brother's also."

"The builder's art is a matter of craft and patience," Siod'h told her. "One does not make stone walls and streets with magic."

"I know that. The craft I can learn, and the patience also."

"First, " he said, "the stones must be moved, the Great Circle must be finished. Then I promise I will come back, and teach you all that I know."

Ryll's eyes were shining, as he had seen Thieras's eyes shine sometimes. What splendors was she imagining?

Then she said, "But there is one other thing . . ."

"Ask it," he said lightly. He could feel the dark thing that had coiled itself round his heart loosening. His thoughts raced ahead with plans, charts, preparations.

"The boy Arun. Send him away, send him back to your Grey Isles."

He turned and stared at her. There was no humor in her face now, no gentleness.

"Alone? He would not last out a day, in this wild country."

"Better that, than to bring down the darkness on all of us. On the people of my mother's and my uncle's tribes."

"Woman, I would not ask you to send one of your maidens away alone, on foot."

"No, you would not. Nor would there be any need to ask it. Siod'h, what a fool you are, what a child! Do you imagine this is some whim of mine, some idle mischief-making? You must understand that no harm will come to him. He will not lose his way, he will not die. It is we who are in mortal danger, every day that he remains among us."

But Siod'h was remembering a wet night in a shepherd's hut, and a red-haired boy half-mad with grief. It was beyond thinking; whatever the reason, he could not tear those two apart again.

Ryll was watching him, seeming to read his thoughts. She shrugged, finally, and said, "Well, twice, three times have I warned you. I can do no more. And I am a greater fool than you, or I should have taken my leave of you long since."

"We have the stones," Siod'h reminded her. "Surely there is power enough there to protect us."

"Listen," Ryll said, "this is the thing you do not understand. While we live in this world, there can be no safety, no protection. Everything in nature moves from order to disorder. If the farmer should leave his barley-field untended for a week, the weeds will spring up and choke the grain. The fields he had cleared with so much labor will in a very short time return to the forest. Look—you are young now, and strong, your flesh is firm. And yet the worm of decay lives in your bones. In this world the darkness is stronger than the light, and chaos more powerful than design. I want no part in a battle I have no hope of winning.''

''Help me to raise the circle,'' Siod'h said, ''and I will show you the true order, the pattern that will stand alone against Chaos, and bind it to man's will.''

At dawn, before the day's labor began, Ryll demanded of her maidens an hour's weapons-practice. Siod'h protested at first, sympathizing with their yawns and their groans as they dragged themselves out of their bedrolls into the chill damp air. ''Have mercy,'' he said, ''they work like dock-laborers, and have earned their rest.''

But Ryll, unrelenting, shook her head. ''I will not have them forget their true craft,'' she said. ''Three years or more, it takes to train a markswoman or a good sword-fighter. Now you would turn them all into gatherers of roots and scourers of pots.''

He watched the slight figures of the women moving like dancers across the hillside: the elegant ritual of thrust and parry, advance, retreat. Thin tendrils of vapor rose from the stony ground, curling serpentlike around their hips. The mist made their shapes seem illusory, insubstantial; it was as though he were watching the specters of some ancient army, long gone to dust.

''As we shall all be soon enough,'' he thought. Ryll gave him an odd look, and he realized that he had spoken aloud. He said, ''I have a sister.''

Ryll raised an inquiring eyebrow.

''She is not yet a woman,'' he said, ''but she has much skill with weapons for so young a maid. You are alike, you and she. If I cannot finish what I have begun, if the end comes too soon . . .''

Ryll put a hand on his shoulder, motioning him to silence.

"Send me the maid," she said. "I will find a place for her. See, here, I will seal the matter." And scratching her wrist with an arrow-point, she began tracing upon the face of a stone the shape of the crescent-moon, her blood-sign. "But you," she said, glancing up. "You carry a sword, but I have not seen you use it." There was pure mischief in her grin. "Nyra," she called out to a dark-haired swordswoman who was catching her breath on the sidelines. "Here is a new partner for you, my girl."

Reluctantly, but seeing no graceful way to refuse, Siod'h drew his sword. He had forgotten when he had last used it. It felt heavy and ill-balanced, as clumsy to the grip as a length of firewood.

Smiling wickedly, Nyra advanced on him with the lithe tread of a mountain-cat, and with catlike ferocity slipped under his awkward guard. In what seemed like an eyeblink her blade-tip was resting gently but firmly against his throat.

Ryll watched in bemusement. "Whatever you learned in that priests' place," she said, "it was not fighting." Then she smiled and put a hand on his arm, to take the edge off her remark.

"There was weapons training," Siod'h admitted. "We were meant to go—if only to clear our heads and work the kinks out of our muscles. But," he finished sheepishly, "in the priests' house they winked at the rule if they thought our time was better spent in study."

"As yours was, clearly. Well, you are not in the priests' house anymore, my friend, and I am making a rule that will not be winked at. From now on I will be your weapons-mistress."

After that she set him to practice every morning for an hour with sword and bow. She was a stern task-mistress. Stiff from the previous day's work, his joints and muscles screamed out for rest; but Ryll, who had labored beside him all day and seemed to draw from an endless fund of energy, gave no quarter.

He stood straight now, with no trace of a scholar's slump. His arms and shoulders grew as firmly muscled as Ryll's.

The timber-crew returned at last, bringing with them an ample supply of rough-dressed oak, and the next stage of the work began.

True to her promise, Ryll had sent for help from her own tribe, and her uncle's tribe, and from two lesser tribes owing fealty to her mother. Many of these were grown men, warriors—thick-set, bearded, silent men, dressed in the skins of deer and marten. But they brought with them also an army of young boys, some as small as eight or ten. The children of the tribes, Ryll said, had little enough to do these lazy warm days, and could better be spared than warriors.

Ryll gave orders with the ease of long-established custom. They moved quickly to her bidding, working in shifts through the long days, from first light to darkness, to build the sleds of squared oak-timbers.

They used forked trunks for the runners, two to a sled, with four struts laid crosswise, and a heavy draw-bar across the front. Even unloaded, the sleds looked hopelessly unwieldy. Siod'h's heart sank, as he saw clearly for the first time the magnitude of his task.

While the carpenters were at work, the rest of the crew was set to digging out the ground beneath the stones, using antler picks, adzes, or whatever tools came to hand, so that the levers could be pushed into place. Finally they were ready to maneuver the stones onto the sleds and lash them down with the heavy ropes of plaited hides.

Even now the stones fought them: two men suffered crushed hands, which needed all of their healing arts to mend. In the night Siod'h and some others awoke, sweating, from dark oppressive dreams.

Now, finally, came the long overland haul, the days of heavy, exhausting labor as they dragged and pushed the stones' huge, clumsy, intractable weight.

The long plaited hauling rcpe was wrapped at intervals

around wooden bars, for easier handholds. On smooth ground the youngest and smallest children were sent ahead with buckets of rendered fat, to grease the roadway. Where the terrain made this impractical, they used rollers, a gang of maidens and young boys darting ceaselessly to and fro to retrieve the logs from behind the sleds and replace them on the track ahead.

The muscles of their arms and shoulders throbbed, ached, eventually went into spasm. Their hands grew at first sore, then raw and bloody. The distance across country was not great—without the weight of the stones to drag, no more than an easy morning's walk. As it was, it meant a five, perhaps six days' journey, working from dawn till after dusk.

With such a great number of mouths to feed they lived off the land, hunting rabbits at dawn and by last light, gathering the summer's bounty of nuts, berries, and greens. Every scrap of animal fat was saved and rendered down to fill the grease-buckets.

Those first nights, as they gathered about the watchfires, their minds were on little but the insistent aches in their backs. They devoured what food they could find, gulped water from the nearest stream, and before it was full dark fell abruptly into sleep.

As they moved down out of the hills onto the open moors the going became easier; here they could slide rather than drag the sleds, down the gentle slopes and over the sparse brown grass. Tireless and noisy as a flock of starlings, the children ran ahead to clear away loose stones and branches.

At night the long shapes bound to the sleds seemed more than ever like dead giants, in whose stone hearts some ghost of life, some stubborn spirit still burned. Ryll's people feared and hated them, building their fires as far away as they could.

On the fifth morning, after two days of intense cloudless heat, they came to the edge of the moors and, following a wide well-marked trail along the banks of a stream, they began to make their way through open larch forest.

It was cooler here, the sun's glare filtered by the feathery pale-green boughs. The air smelled pleasantly of ferns and moss. Like an invading army they drove deeper into the wood, shattering the silence with shouts, songs, groans, curses, and the incessant tortured creaking of the sleds.

The brief time between twilight and full dark was the hour for the bone-dice, for songs of old battles and old kings, for storytelling. That first night in the larch forest, drugged by fatigue and the fire's warmth, Siod'h lay back in something very near to contentment.

An owl called softly in the purple gloom. One of the women, for a joke, hooted back at it.

"Do not mock the owl," a comrade admonished her. "She serves our Lady of the Trees."

A man from the Grey Isles said, "There are some folk believe the owl is a bird of ill omen, that warns us of our deaths."

Arun, who had been sitting alone while he waited for Bryn to finish sentry duty, was heard to remark, mysteriously, "They say that of the crane also."

Siod'h and some others glanced at the boy with mild surprise, so unaccustomed were any of them to hear him speak. But now, for some reason, Arun seemed disposed to break his long silence.

"I dreamed that the owl and the crane came to me," he said. "I was near to dying, and they led me back to life."

Siod'h felt an odd thrill of expectancy. Under cover of darkness he moved closer to the boy.

"Clearly, there is a tale to be told there," he said softly. "Tell me, have you made a song of it?"

Arun turned to stare at him, and in the fire's glare Siod'h could see the hesitation, the bewilderment in his eyes. Suddenly, like a pent-up stream, the words spilled out.

"I was in a dark place," he said. "A sea-cave. I smelled salt, and sea weed, and cold wet stone. I felt nothing— neither cold nor wet nor pain; and being blind also in the darkness, I thought that I was drowned. Then I felt something brushing softly against my face. I opened my eyes—I had not known that they were tight-shut before. I looked up, then, and saw a great white crane, whose feathers shone like moonlight in the dark. It touched me with its beak, and I knew that I must get up and follow it. I was not, after all, dead, it seemed—I could feel, and see, and after a time my arms and legs, that had been stiff and moveless as a corpse's limbs, regained their strength.

"I got up, and followed the crane. It led me, not out of the cave's mouth, but through many narrow passageways, deeper and deeper into the heart of the cliff.

"After walking for what seemed an hour or more, I emerged upon the other side. I thought that I must have slept for a very long time, as one who is under a spell; for what lay upon the far side of the cliff was a winter forest, with the glimmer of frost upon the ground, and the trees standing black and leafless against the sky.

"I could not see the crane anywhere—it had vanished away into the dark. But now there flew before me a silver-feathered owl, that hooted softly and made me understand that I should follow, as I had followed the crane. It flew on before me. White as moonlight it was, against those skeletal branches.

"We came out of the forest, and all at once the winter and the night had vanished, and the warmth of summer lay upon the land. Before me was a broad green meadow, scattered with flowers. I could see in the far distance a gleam of walls and lime-white towers.

"I heard the thud of hooves upon the grass, and saw riding toward me a young man, of princely bearing. His tunic was cloth-of-gold, and his cloak of yellow silk. Like silk too was his yellow hair, hanging loose and shining upon his shoulders."

Arun broke off, glancing anxiously out into the dark at the edge of the camp; and they all knew it was time for the watch to change. Presently Bryn appeared, whistling, and sprawled at Arun's side.

He showed no surprise as Arun picked up the thread of his story. Siod'h guessed that for Bryn, at least, it was a twice-told tale.

"He bade me leap up behind him, on his great white stallion. And we rode away over the flowering meadow toward those distant towers.

"Along the road grew trees of gold and silver, hung with crystal fruits; their branches stirring in the soft wind made a sweet music, like the tinkling of many chimes.

"Of white bronze was the palace built, and great blocks of blue and green and amethyst crystal. The colors shimmered and flowed together like the colors of a sunlit sea. The doors of hammered silver were thrown wide in welcome; sweet music wafted from within, and the smell of flowers."

Arun smiled to himself, remembering. "How can I describe to you the enchantment of that place? What shall I say of the men and women who dwelt there? How gentle they were, how graceful; innocent in their pleasures as children, careless of the riches that surrounded them; careless too of their own flawless beauty. To feasting and to music they devoted all their days, and their nights, to love.

"And yet in the midst of it all, I felt a great restlessness, a longing for my own country, my own kin. And I remembered tales of men and women who had visited the lands of faerie for but a single day, and yet returning, found their friends and their loved ones had grown old, and died.

"And I feared that I should never see you again, my brother. I went to the prince of that land, who had brought me thither, and asked him to show me the way back to my own country. He chided me, in that gentle way of his, for spurning their company; and all the ladies of the court pleaded with me to change my mind. But in the end I had my way. They gave me wine to drink, and presently I woke—knowing I had slept, and dreamed—on the cold sand of the shore."

"But," someone asked, "how did you find your way back to your friends?"

"Ah," said Arun, "that is no mystery. How does the salmon find its way to the river's mouth, or the seabird to its own nest? The road lay plain before me."

Siod'h heard Bryn laugh—a pleased, contented sound. A thousand questions leaped into Siod'h's head, but he left them for another time, telling himself, maybe it was as the boy had said—he had fallen asleep in the wet sand, and dreamed of enchantment.

But across the dying fire, he felt Ryll's quiet gaze upon him, and he could not meet her eyes.

On the morrow, it was slow, hard going; the sun in its swift westward progress mocked their labors. According to Siod'h's map they should by now have reached the banks of a river, but as they pushed on, their track instead grew narrower and rougher—dwindling by late afternoon to a dim passageway through tangled oakwoods.

Knotted roots crawled over the path, impeding the sleds; a work-party had to be sent ahead to clear the way with axes.

Bryn glanced nervously over his shoulder. "I mislike this place," he said. "It puts me too much in mind of a certain other wood." The thought was clear enough, though left unspoken—"It is not where I would choose to spend the night."

"You've seen the charts," Siod'h replied, his voice edged with sudden irritation. Hunger and fatigue were making them all quick-tempered. "The river cannot be far—an hour or so at most."

"Look ahead," Ynas said. "It seems lighter there—maybe we are nearing the end of it."

But the light was a false hope—not the riverbank, after all, but only a narrow glade, a stony place, in the middle of the wood. Beyond was deeper forest, a place of perpetual twilight, that seemed to go on to the world's end.

No trees grew here but the immense primordial oaks, their trunks gnarled and twisted by centuries of cramped sunless growth. Mistletoe ran riot; moss straggled down from the branches, long and pale as old men's beards. Beside the path lay huge broken boulders and decaying oak-limbs. Moss-shrouded, their shapes were vague and mysterious in the gloom.

"This is an evil place," the woman Creidah suddenly burst out. She was peering fearfully into the shadows, ready to bolt at the snapping of a twig.

"Be silent," Ryll said sharply. "That is foolish talk, and I will hear no more of it." But, thought Siod'h, there was not much conviction in her voice.

They had come out into a large bracken-filled clearing, walled by darkness. "We'll camp here," Siod'h said.

He looked back along the trail, at the long double line of men, women, and children straggling away into the shadows. They were seizing the chance to rest from their labors—rubbing their sore backs and arms, and muttering uneasily to themselves.

Was there ever, thought Siod'h, a general less certain of his command? What reason had any of these frightened and exhausted people to follow him? What words of comfort or inspiration could he offer them? Ehlreth would have known the right words. He longed suddenly and fiercely for that gentle, infinitely reassuring presence.

To Creidah, finally, he said, "This place is not evil. In nature there is only order, and disorder. It is indifferent to our little notions of good and evil, that exist only in our own heads."

"Be that as it may," added Ryll, 'there is no turning back now. We must make the best of it."

They gathered wood and lit the watchfires, huddling close to the warmth and light. Yet with the leaping flames came none of the ease, the peace that one feels in one's own hearth-place. The walls of the night leaned in upon them; the rising smoke made queer shapes among the trees.

No one, it seemed, escaped that sense of danger, of ill omen. A shapeless, lurking fear it was, that knotted the belly and parched the throat. The children wailed miserably, and refused to lie down; the adults, speaking anxiously in whispers, comforted the smallest ones as best they could.

Ryll, or perhaps one of her maidens, heard it first—the ears of the hill-bred women were marvelously acute. The whole camp was quiet then, listening. The sound in itself was nothing ominous—merely a soft rustling and brushing, as of some large animal moving through the underbrush. But then there came a scream choked off, abruptly as a door shutting; and there followed a silence that was more dreadul than any sound.

Out of some deep abyss of time they rode—the powers of darkness, winter, age, and death. Stone-grey were their cloaks and the leather of their boots; their helms and their harness-studs had a dark oily sheen, like slate. Grey, too, were their horses—the pale luminous color of mist.

At their heels, like a great pack of hounds, ran the demon-swine, the black and brindled great-crested boars. Huge and deadly were their tusks, like curving knives. Their eyes were blood-red and glaring; from out of their immense maws there foamed and dripped a bloody slaver.

So close now were those grey stallions that Siod'h could have put out a hand and touched their gleaming flanks. The riders had thrown back their helms—and seeing the spectral features beneath, he shuddered. Their skins too, were grey—grey as the very countenance of death. Their eyes had the dull grey shine of stones on a winter beach. About each of those faces—the set of the eyes, the shape of the brow and jaw—there was something that was subtly distorted and perverse.

Around him in the darkness Siod'h sensed swift, purposeful movement—knives sliding out of belts, arrows drawn from quivers. Then abruptly, Ryll ordered her people back.

"Put down your weapons," she said. "This is no battle of ours—though we may die of it all the same."

At that instant there crashed from out of cover a monstrous brindled boar, a creature near to a man's height at the chest, with tusks thick as oak-limbs, long and sharp as spears.

As it advanced, the great head swung slowly from side to side; the eyes, red as hot coals, searched feverishly among the shadows.

A cry rang out, filled with such terror that hearing it, the heart froze. It was the sound of one who, suddenly and without forewarning, looks into the naked face of death. That voice, as they all guessed at once, belonged to Arun.

Somewhere in the shadows a bow-string twanged; an arrow, sure-aimed and deadly, whined past Siod'h and buried itself in the monster's throat. It was not the small bolt the hillsmen used, but the long grey-fletched arrow of the Isles.

The boar paused for no more than a second in its headlong plunge, shook its great head as though a fly buzzed at its ears, and then veered sideways. It peered into the darkness, searching for its tormentor. The huge clumsy body lurched forward, the head tossed. There was a glint of white tusks in the firelight, a shout of sudden agony, choked off, then silence.

The boar scraped at the mossy ground with its forefeet, watching Arun with its small malevolent eyes. One of its tusks was smeared with blood.

Now, in the distance still but drawing steadily closer, they could hear the high-pitched mournful baying of hounds— first one, then many, as the whole pack took up the cry.

Like the grey lords, these riders came in silence, save for the hounds' baying; their heads bare, their long hair streaming back from their pale, high brows. Their eyes glowed blue as witchfire in that dark place; their faces were both stern and beautiful.

In the awe and terror of that moment, Siod'h felt as though he were looking upon some artist's vision that sears the mind, the eye, with a truth more vivid and more real than life; every detail leaping out as though illuminated by a lightning flash.

The leader looked down briefly and met Siod'h's gaze; his eyes washed Siod'h's face in pale blue fire.

His cloak was deep crimson, falling back in heavy folds from a golden torque, over a yellow silk tunic embroidered with threads of gold. He bore two silver spears with rivets of bronze, and a great sword, golden-hilted, golden-studded. His shield was crimson with a silver rim. At his heels ran three snow-white hounds with eyes and ears of flame.

All this Siod'h saw in an eye's blink, in the space of a heartbeat: vivid as a poppy-dream, yet tangible as his own solid flesh.

Suddenly, a great battle-cry broke the stillness. The golden-hilted sword lifted, the white stallion reared and plunged forward, lashing out with golden hooves.

The brindled boar shook its vast head in dull-minded bewilderment. It backed slowly away from Arun, and swung round to face the Lord of Light.

Siod'h caught one glimpse of Arun's frozen, huge-eyed face; and then, trailing yellow fire, the golden sword rose and fell, cutting through swineflesh as though it were soft cheese, and burying itself to the hilt in the black chest. The boar sank to its knees and toppled sideways; it shuddered once, enormously, and died.

All this was accomplished in the space of time it took the grey riders to rein in, and wheel their mounts about. Now, their faces black with anger, they snapped down their visors, lifted their great swords, and plunged straight into the ranks of Faerie.

The silence was broken by the dull thunder of hooves, the ring of metal on metal, the screams of terrified horses and wounded hounds. Bushes were trampled, watchfires scattered in the fury of the combat; birds flew up shrieking out of the midnight wood. Blows were struck that should have sliced through muscle and bone, severed limbs from trunks, split skulls asunder; yet not one rider fell beneath the flailing hooves, and no blood ran. For all the fierceness of the encounter, it was curiously like the battle-dances one saw sometimes at court: those re-enactments, by acrobats and actors, of ancient wars.

Siod'h felt Ryll's hand resting gently on his shoulder.

"You see," she said, "that war must go on to world's end, since death has no power to finish it. It is like a board-game, with all the fallen pieces set up again at the close of play. Friend, do you see now what forces you have chosen to meddle with?"

Those who, like Siod'h, had courage to watch, observed this also: that although the grey lords attacked with a bitter and brutal ferocity, in this battle at least they were no match for the warriors of Faerie. Little by little, mercilessly, they were driven back, by a force as subtle and sure as it was deadly. In the end, cursing and howling, graceless in their defeat, they turned and fled.

As the riders of Faerie gathered up their reins and made ready to depart, their leader rode forward, straight to the tree behind which Arun had sought shelter.

Huge and beautiful as the sun, his equipage glowing in its own yellow light, he looked down at the boy, and then, wordlessly, reached out a gloved hand to pull him up. They saw Arun smile, his eyes wide and marveling as a child's; they saw him hook his fingers into the rider's sword-belt and lean close against that broad crimson-cloaked back. The two rode off. After a time a horn sounded, faint and eerie on the damp night air.

They found Bryn lying in a pool of crimson that had spread beneath him like a cloak. Red foam flecked his lips. His eyes were wide open, staring with a puzzled hurt. His red hair looked startling as flames against his chalk-white face. The spear of the boar-tusk had pierced his chest, driving through muscle and ribcage, into the lung. A great wound, beyond the reach of healing magic.

Ynas was kneeling beside the boy. "Arun has gone home," Siod'h heard him whisper. "Now you must go to meet him, he is waiting for you."

Bryn was too weak from shock and loss of blood to answer. But the puzzlement faded, and a look almost of contentment came over his face. Soon after that he closed his eyes, and died.

They buried Bryn with what ceremony they could, laying him under a cairn of mossy stones, while Ryll's maidens sang the lament.

They did not speak of him, or of Arun, again.

With the first light they left that haunted place, and before the mists had cleared they had left the deep woods behind them. They came to the banks of a shallow, swift-running river, winding its way south among hawthorn and hazel scrub. They followed it downstream until, flowing through meadowlands and sunny woods, it widened and deepened.

Here, among scattered stands of pine, hazel, and holly, they made their camp, and began the building of the rafts.

Daily Siod'h consulted the sheepskin scroll upon which he marked out his calendar, and daily was reassured that it was high summer still, that time remained to him. Yet, looking up at the steep woods overhanging their valley, he saw that there was already a tinge of red and gold along the higher slopes. Once the sun was down, he could feel in the air the bite of autumn. The winter, when it came, would be a hard one—not the mild open season he had prayed for.

He set the youngest children to gathering nuts and berries, thus freeing the adults for the heavier work of raft-building. With a plentiful supply of timber near at hand, the work went quickly.

Drawn up on the riverbank, the rafts looked immense and awkward. They launched one, unloaded, and found that, once afloat, the three layers of lashed pine-logs rode almost on the water's surface.

They were four days moving the stones from the sleds to the rafts, and a day in the launching. The long line of rafts, lying low in the water now under the great weight of the stones, slid effortlessly down-river.

The tide was on the ebb as they reached the estuary, exposing a wide expanse of mudflats and salt-marshes. Everywhere there were waterfowl, wading on their thin legs among the slimed rocks of the shore. In the yellow light of late afternoon the rafts floated out into the placid waters of the Haven.

Ynas had left the dugouts in the care of some fisherfolk, with the promise of silver on his return. He was relieved, all the same, to find the boats undisturbed.

Ryll's women, who earlier had waded off into the reed-beds, returned with enough birds to feed the camp. The children, full-bellied at last and in a holiday mood, splashed and cavorted among the rafts like seal-pups.

That night Siod'h drew Ryll aside to make his farewells. Though some of the hill-people had agreed to make the voyage along the coast, she herself feared salt water, she said; and besides, she must return her maidens to their village in time for the harvest-rites.

"And when will you return?" she asked him.

"It must be before the snows come," Siod'h replied, "or never."

"And you will bring me the child, your sister?"

"If I can. Or else send her."

There was a wicked glint in Ryll's eyes as she said, "It is to be hoped that your swordsmanship does not run in the family."

"I think not," he assured her with mock seriousness. "I believe that is my own achievement entirely."

She grinned, then went on more soberly, "When I am back at my village, I will offer a white goat to the World-Mother for your safe journey—and your safe return.''

He was touched by that, and a little surprised, till he remembered her dreams of cities, and his promise. Then, just as they were parting, she reached out and touched his arm.

"Never mind what I said about your swordsmanship," she told him. "Anybody can be taught to fight—with a little patience. What matters only is that you have the heart for it. And in truth, friend, you were born with more than your share of courage.'' She smiled, and added softly, "I will look for you, then, before the snows come.''

At dawn, as they left the Haven, the sun rose huge and yellow out of the east, like a beacon; the sea lay smooth as glass in the dry, windless air.

Shepherded by the dugouts, the rafts moved out from the Haven in two long rows. Given calm seas, the wind and current would carry them eastward along the coast, all the way to the mouth of the Hefryn. Yet Siod'h dreaded this part of the journey, fearing the havoc a storm might wreak on the heavily laden vessels.

Wary by now of hidden rocks and the treacherous currents around the headlands, he ordered the raftsmen to steer well clear of the shore. Beyond that, he told himself, they must trust the tide, the following wind, and the gods.

In the event, their luck held; or maybe after all Ryll's white goat had bought their safety. Driven shoreward by a gale that sprang up toward nightfall, they beached their fleet on a long sloping stretch of sand between two cliffs. Not a single vessel was lost. Ponderous and clumsy as the rafts were, they had proven their seaworthiness: impossible to swamp, they lumbered stolidly through the wildest weather.

They lay up on the beach for two days while the storm raged, huddled in cloaks and skins in the lee of the rafts. The islanders prayed to the Sea-Lady, and Ryll's people to their hill-gods; when at last the wind died and the sun broke through, it seemed their prayers had been answered. The fine weather held all the way to the mouth of the Hefryn.

They entered that broad grey tideway, sweeping in on the flood through miles of desolate flatlands, webbed by streams and narrow tidal inlets.

The current bore them swiftly inland, between low red cliffs and crumbling mud-banks, with forest beyond, and so on to the confluence of the Hefryn and the Green-willow.

Presently they found themselves in pleasant meadow-country. Willows and poplars fringed the gently sloping banks; beyond, in the yellowing fields, dog-roses bloomed.

Still farther on, the river narrowed and curved through the steep cliffs of Greenwillow Gorge. Before they reached that narrow place, the stones would be transferred to shallow-drafted riverboats. From there, under Ynas's command, the stones must travel up the Greenwillow and its tributaries, overland to the headwaters of the Winterbourne, and thence through the chalklands to the temple site. Though it was a tedious journey, there was nothing dangerous or even difficult about it. Those inland rivers swarmed with boats, and downsmen eager to work for Island silver.

"Look there," said the novice Leu, shading his eyes against the glare of sun on water. "There is the meeting place. I can see the boats, scores of them, all along the bank." His voice shook with excitement.

A great crowd of men and women stood shouting and waving at the river's edge; among them was a certain gawky, dark-haired child. Siod'h leaped off the raft, reached shallow water, splashed over a sandbar and through some reeds, and scrambled up the bank. A shape hurled itself upon him, clutching him fiercely.

"We waited and waited," said a small voice, thick with tears. "We waited and watched and still you did not come." He rubbed his cheek against Mara's hair; it smelled of woodsmoke, and wild roses.

"It was a greater task than we knew," he said. "Remember, I only said that I would come. Never did I name the day, or the week, even. Anyway," he said, untangling himself and holding her at arm's length, "we are here, and for now the waiting is behind us."

"For now?"

Could he have forgotten how quick she was to seize on a word, a look even, and read from that the whole of one's secret mind?

"But surely, now, you are finished?"

"Listen to me, little hawk." He pulled her down beside him, into the willow-shade. "You cannot imagine the weight of these stones, the power that holds them rooted to the earth. To move them is like tearing an oak tree out of rock, or an organ out of living flesh. In the night I used to dream that the stones had mouths, that screamed curses when I touched them." He looked down at his scarred and calloused hands. "The work is not finished. We have done what we could, but it is not enough to complete the circle."

"But you, you must stay here to see the stones erected?"

He shook his head. "The priests will see to that. I have given Ehlreth the plans. Time is short, and I must finish what I have begun. And anyway, there are promises I must keep, in the wild lands—to those who helped me."

He could see that she was fighting to hold back tears. "Listen well, little sister," he said. "Do you still mean to be a warrior?"

She nodded, her grey eyes puzzled.

"Then so be it. I must go back to the wild lands, but this time you shall have your wish—I will take you with me. There is a woman there, a princess of the high country, and a great warrior. She has said that she will take you into her care, and train you."

A grey light blazed suddenly in her eyes. She hugged herself, and then Siod'h, in astonished joy.

"But understand, little one, that there is no turning back.

When I return to the Grey Isles, you must remain behind, in the wild lands.''

"But," she said, and her face was alive still with eagerness, "when the circle is finished, and the Old Gods are bound, then you will come for me, will you not? To be a warrior in my own country?"

There was a silence, filled only by the small sounds of the river sucking and churning among the weeds.

She was waiting. There was only one answer he could give her. "Yes," he said presently. "I will come for you. If I finish the circle, if the binding holds . . . if the sea spares us. Then I will come. You have my promise.''

She stared at him—hearing, as always, not the words but the thought lying hidden behind them. Understanding too much.

Her mouth trembled; another child might have wept, but she only shrugged one thin shoulder and grinned crookedly up at him. "Try not to be too long," was all she said.

He smiled at that, thinking how much she sounded like Ryll. It would satisfy his sense of pattern, to bring those two together.

And remembering all that must be done, before that happened—what plans made, what maps and charts drawn up, what orders given—his thoughts, like the tide through the gorge, leaped purposefully ahead.

THE
LAST SONG

Ainn

Overcast though the day was, there had been no rain for a fortnight; maybe that was why the air seemed thick with dust. No matter how thoroughly Ainn cleaned, in the mornings everything—floors, tables, dishes—was covered with a fine grey powder. She would have given it up as a waste of time, but for the need to keep occupied. She had been a mind-healer long enough to know the value of work as a remedy for black moods.

Her cousin the High King had chided her once, arriving unannounced to find her on her knees with a scrub brush, a scarf wrapped round her hair and an old gown kilted into her girdle.

"Surely, Ainn," he had said, "you could find a servant to do that."

She had laughed at him. He was a good, kind man; but inclined to be pompous.

"What use have I for a servant?" she had asked him, as she ushered him into her dayroom, a chamber as small and sparsely furnished as a priest's.

Watching the dust settle back on the freshly washed steps, Ainn wondered if perhaps it was a sign, like the falling stars, the strange lights at sea, the earth's trembling. That was something she would have to ask Ehlreth. She had never trained in augury; there had always seemed more than enough to concern her in the present.

Remembering that she had not eaten since morning, she ladled some fish soup out of the hearth-kettle; but after a few mouthfuls she pushed aside her bowl. She had not had much taste for food, of late. This disturbed her a little, when she thought about it. Until now she had always enjoyed a robust appetite.

Well, she thought, as frugally she tipped the rest of the soup back into the kettle, it must just be a sign that I am growing old. Like the small aches and twinges, the stiffness in her hip when she climbed the stairs, or those grim days when she could not seem to shake off the grip of melancholy.

As she set off down the beach toward the causeway, a flock of herring-gulls followed her, their bright greedy eyes curious. Poor creatures, she thought. Living under her protection, they had grown fat and lazy. She wondered if they would manage to fly to safety when the time came.

Westward, over the shadowed cliffs of the Sorcerers' Isle, a low sun broke through, edging the clouds with gold. Ainn's spirits lifted a little. It was the endless succession of grey days that had weighed so heavily upon her.

Just above the tideline was a small circle of stones, a scattering of charred sticks. A beachfire. Her sleep was often broken, these nights, by loud laughter and singing. The revelers came, for the most part, from the town—sons and daughters of merchants and artisans, entertainers from the Flower Courts; but among them she had seen children of the great families, her own blood kin.

The music and the shouting were no matter, and would not have disturbed her. The young had always behaved so—it was the way of nature, a joyful thing, and essentially innocent. But sometimes she woke in the dark of her room with all her nerves crawling, her hair prickling on her scalp. Those were the the times when, listening, she heard that the music had changed, had become a rhythmic and insistent chanting, with the beat of drums behind it. On one such night she had gone to her seaward window and looked out: had seen, black against the leaping flames, the shapes of things that were neither human, nor in any proper sense alive.

She thrust that memory from her. Seeking tranquility, she imagined her mind as a still deep lake; her thoughts, like small silver fishes, gliding gently just beneath the surface.

"As in order there is serenity, so with serenity comes perfect order."

She had forgotten the name of the old priest who had said that, when she was a novice of fourteen, all nerves and awkward limbs and over-eagerness. She had never forgotten the maxim.

She reached the Sorcerers' Isle just at sundown, and started up the cliff-path. Halfway to the top she looked back and saw the sea spread out below her like a sheet of silver, divided by the straight black line of the causeway. Low on the horizon the clouds were stained a luminous apricot-pink.

This, like the dawn, was the Lady's time, the moment when her presence was most clearly seen, and felt. In that communion, brief though it might be, was strength and comfort.

Ainn came to the temple and pushed open the great doors, observing with pleasure and gratitude that sudden white burst of radiance. Here at least, in the Great Hall, the ancient charms held: order and custom had been maintained.

But in the back passages, among the warrens of cells, the dust lay thick as eider down. By now most of the novices had been sent across water, to the safety of the hills, and the temple-servants had gone with them.

As she walked along the corridors the peculiar smell of the priests' house—that mingling of dust and damp stone, lamp-oil and vellum—recalled with a sudden poignancy her own time as initiate and adept. Memories rushed in upon her—cats asleep in pools of sunlight on the flagstones; the drone of novices learning their formulae by rote; cold winter afternoons by the library hearth; the deep enduring quiet of the place.

Here, always, past and present were indivisible: a thousand generations of the priesthood, reaching out across time as well as distance, linked by the changeless laws, the unbroken lines of knowledge.

Though some of the younger priests still labored over their charts in the grey light, the cells of the magi and archimagi were deserted. Knowing at once where they had gone, Ainn followed them down the long uncarpeted corridor to the library.

This large, homely, cluttered room had from earliest days been the heart of the temple, and their favorite gathering place. Here, on plank shelves, on benches and tables, were stored sheepskins, tablets of clay and stone, atlases, star-maps, charts of ocean currents, records dating back into antiquity. Ainn remembered it as a place of silence—or, in the long evenings, of quiet fireside talk. Tonight the hush was shattered by a dozen voices raised in heated argument.

Discussion had always been the lifeblood of the place. In the eyes of the temple—in matters of science at least—all theses were possible, all points of view worthy of consideration. Yet in these voices, tonight, she detected a new and sharper note of discord.

As she came into the room the cosmologist Jabath held the floor. "I tell you," he was saying, in his dry old man's voice, "there is nothing of the supernatural here. According to my calculations, and those of Breac and Maol"—he nodded acknowledgment to the temple's chief astrologers—"we are in the path of a wandering star which is exerting a malign and powerful influence upon us. Just as the moon governs the flow of the tides, so now will this erratic body disturb both the movement of the oceans and of the earth itself, causing a vast upheaval of the waters and a fracturing and shifting of the rocks within the earth."

"Let me remind you," said Maol, taking up the thread of the argument, "of the visit of the tailed star recorded during the reign of the High King Ellwynd. It was said to be larger than the sun, and so brilliant that it lit up the sky by both day and night. Abnormally high tides were recorded, and there were great windstorms and violent earth tremors."

But Fatha the geomancer was shaking his head. "If true, it was a coincidence," he said. "In that same reign and the one following it, there were recorded no fewer than four periods of climatic disturbances, earthquakes, and flooding of coastal cities. It is not the movements of the stars that causes these disruptions, but rather the breaking of the earth-web— the natural lines of force that serve to bind the forces of disorder."

"Ah, but the reason . . ." said Aedha the mathematician. "The reason lies deeper still. What force has broken the earth-web? What but the waking of the Old Gods, the faceless ones?"

"But," pointed out the oceanographer Kermath, "according to the auguries, it is not the earth but the sea that will destroy us."

"Earth, sea, stars . . ." said Aedha. His bass voice made of those three words a litany of doom. "Do you not understand, it is the Lords of Chaos who are fighting among themselves, each one striving for mastery? What does it matter in the end who conquers—the lords of the rocks, or the undersea, or the outer dark? Whichever wins, we are the losers. That is an unalterable equation."

No, thought Ainn with sudden anger. Not that, surely. Not unalterable. Must all that passion of debate be reduced in the end to cynical acceptance? Bitterly she recalled her own words to Thieras: "It will come. There is not power enough in all these isles to stop it. Too many have lost faith, have forsaken the hard path."

But Siod'h had not lost faith. Even now, on the Great Down, they were raising the blue stones; and Siod'h had gone back into the wilderness, because he believed—against all commonsense, all logic, that the circle could be finished.

She saw the face she had been seeking; quietly she crossed the room. Ehlreth smiled and made room for her on his bench. He said nothing, only took her hand, holding it lightly in his own.

"Do they always go on like this?" she whispered.

"Lately, yes."

"Surely," she said, "their time would be better spent in building our defenses."

"How fierce you sound," he said in amusement. "Like Thieras."

"Exactly. There is another who will not so easily admit defeat."

"No," he said gently. "This one time, Ainn, I think you are mistaken. The work goes on. But at the end of the day when the mind is weary and resolution flags, it is not a bad thing to meet like this."

"Only to argue?"

"Especially to argue. Do you remember old Cimbraith?"

She shook her head. "By reputation, only. He died before my time."

"Well, he used to say that where men still had the will to argue, to defend with passion any idea, no matter how foolish, then true despair could not take root."

She looked down at her folded hands. "On the beach," she said, "I have seen dark things raised out of the night."

"Necromancy?" She nodded. "Among other practices. It

began in the Flower Courts with the minstrel, the one they say lost his voice to Faerie.''

"Ainn, you know this man, and as a theurge you must understand the powers he is meddling with.''

"Yes,'' she said, "I know him. I ought to,'' she added wryly, "he is a relative of mine. But no, do not ask me to interfere. I have spoken to him. Enough to know that reason, argument, threats—all are futile. And besides, he is not alone. These things spread like the choking-sickness. Well,'' she said, "none of this is what I meant to say to you. What I came to ask was only this: how much time do you believe is left?''

"If I were you,'' Ehlreth said, "I would ask Aedha that question. He is the one who deals in figures and equations.''

She smiled at that. The gentle irony in Ehlreth's voice had not escaped her.

"I work with dreams, with visions,'' he said. "Of all the sciences, mine is the least exact.''

"All the same,'' said Ainn, "though I am neither a mathematician nor a seer, I can tell that the sand is running out of the glass. Well, we will leave that question for the moment . . . and I will ask another. Tell me if Siod'h's work will succeed, if he will finish the circle.''

Ehlreth said, "I could give you an answer I once gave Thieras. I could say, truthfully enough, that what I see are probabilities; that anything remains possible.''

As he spoke, he had been staring into the fire; now he turned his head, and what she saw in his face was answer enough. He gripped her hand, hard. "My dear Ainn, why must I say this, when you will read my thoughts anyway? Well, to you I will say what seems to me now, a certainty— that Siod'h will fail.''

She accepted that, with a sudden sharp grief: more for Siod'h than for themselves.

"Then listen,'' she said after a moment. "When Thieras came to me, seeking comfort, I told her this: that there was not magic enough in the temple, not magic enough in all the Grey Isles, to hold the sea back. It seemed to me true enough, when I said it. An unalterable equation. But Ehlreth, ours is not the only temple. There are others over-water, on the downs, in the hills, along the coast . . . everywhere that our people have settled. Remember—you must have learned it as a novice—'After a thousand thousand generations, the sorcerers' blood runs true.' ''

Ehlreth made as if to speak, but waited, seeing that she was not finished.

"I am going over-water," she said. "To the high downs, where Siod'h's temple is."

"Alone?" In the end, that was all that he asked her.

She shook her head. "I will ask Thieras to go with me. I owe her that much. And if indeed we have only a little time left, I would as soon spend it with her, as with anyone."

"I will tell you," Ehlreth said, "when it is time." And then he added, "It will not be long."

The message came sooner than either of them had expected: not on that night, nor on the next, but on the third night thereafter. Well past midnight, Ainn was shaken awake by a violent shuddering and lurching of the floor. At the same time there came an enormous and terrifying sound: a grinding and rumbling that seemed to be everywhere at once—in the air, in the ground itself.

All of it—the noise, the shaking of the earth—was over in seconds, though it seemed to last far longer. An immense silence fell, broken only by the cries of seabirds rudely awakened in their nests. In the midst of her fright and bewilderment Ainn heard Ehlreth's voice speaking clearly in her mind.

"It is time," the voice said.

She went to the narrow window of her bedchamber and looked out. There to the west, a shower of stars was falling like bright rain through the moonless air.

Ainn shivered, and hugged herself; creeping back into her bed, she dozed fitfully until an hour or so before dawn.

With the first grey light she rose, dressed, splashed water on her face, ate a handful of biscuits. Then she packed into a pouch some hardcake and smoked meat, her tinder and sky-stone, and a few packets of herbs. She put a good bronze knive into her girdle, and rolled a change of clothing into a heavy blanket. This done, she set out for the King's House, to rouse Thieras.

She entered the Great House uninvited and unannounced. The sentry's hair and tunic were rumpled; she suspected he had been asleep, before the tremor struck. Certainly he was wide awake now. He seemed unsurprised by her visit, early as the hour was.

Though she had half expected to find the whole house astir, the corridors were dark and silent. There had been many smaller tremors these past weeks; perhaps people were growing accustomed to them.

Thieras's room was small, neat, uncluttered. A lamp still burned on a table near the bed. Linen curtains stirred in the draft through the open window.

Thieras lay curled under a counterpane, her arms wrapped around her pillow, her dark hair fanned out in a shining circle.

Ainn whispered her name, and shook her gently awake. She rolled over and sat up, all in one swift motion, her eyes wide and startled. In her high-necked white nightdress, with her hair falling loose on her shoulders, she looked more child than woman.

"Ainn? Is it happening, then?" Thieras sounded, not afraid exactly, but surprised and apprehensive.

"Not yet. It is only that I have a journey to make, and I wanted your company."

"Journey?" Thieras was half-asleep still. She repeated the word slowly, as though perplexed by its meaning.

"Over-water, to the mainland. No, lass," Ainn added quickly, understanding Thieras's look. "I am not running away, any more than you are. But it is time to call our people together. I mean to build a wall against the sea."

Thieras asked no more questions. She threw back the covers and reached for her clothes.

It was a grey morning, promising rain. By the time they reached the shore a fine drizzle was falling, the first in weeks.

"Look there," said Thieras. Through the thin mist along the shore a figure was approaching.

"Hawkmaid!" the man called out, when they were within hailing distance.

"It's Eirech," Thieras said. Ainn had a great urge to turn back—to pretend neither to have seen nor heard; but he was their kinsman, and in common courtesy they must greet him.

Bareheaded and cloakless in the raw air, Eirech was dressed as though he had just come from a feast. At his throat he wore a silver collar of twined serpents with glittering amethyst eyes. His tunic and hose were of some fine silvery fabric—rumpled now, and badly water-spotted. There was a faint shadow of beard on his cheeks and jaw.

In spite of herself Ainn was shocked by his appearance. He was thinner, almost haggard-looking, and that lithe dancer's grace she remembered had become mere affectation, a self-conscious and uneasy posturing. His eyes looked veiled, opaque. She had seen that look before.

"Hawkmaid," he said to Thieras, "since last we met, you have grown older—and wiser in the world's ways, I think." His speech was slurred, a little. Something glittered in his eyes—a ghost of that old ironic wit—though all the grace had gone out of it, leaving only a hard malice.

"I thought our handsome cousin Dhan might have had a hand in that—but seeing you two together, it occurs to me, perhaps the lady has other tastes."

Ainn felt the younger woman stiffen, felt something grow tight and hard in Thieras's mind, a knot of cold rage like a clenched fist.

"Softly," Ainn murmured. "Girl, he is not worth your anger." She took Thieras's arm and drew her away. Eirech's laughter followed them down the beach—a shrill, high sound, edged with madness.

Muffled in their cloaks, they rowed out of the harbor. The tide was with them, and the wind was out of the east. Toward mid-morning the sky cleared and the sun came out, flooding with vivid light the grey headlands and the narrow beaches of yellow sand.

"Remember," said Thieras, "how I taught Siod'h to climb after gulls' eggs, and how frightened he was at first?" They were rounding a promontory, high limestone cliffs that fell sharply to the sea.

"Well I remember," said Ainn, shivering. "What a wild, willful creature you were then. I would see the pair of you scrambling on hands and knees on the sea-cliffs, and not draw an easy breath till you were safely down again. They named you well, hawkmaid."

Thieras laughed. "It's in the blood," she said. "My little cousin Mara—though she's not so little now—she's another of the same breed."

Ainn glanced up suddenly. "Did they tell you, Mara has gone back into the wild lands with Siod'h?" She saw by Thieras's look that she hadn't known.

"There is a warrior-woman there, who has taken her into training."

"I will miss her," Thieras said. "She used to tag after me like a small shadow when I went rabbiting. I meant this summer to choose a falcon for her." Thieras's face clouded. "I had forgotten that. I'm sorry now, she should have had a bird of her own, she was ready for it." She shrugged. "Anyway, I am glad she has gone with Siod'h. That eager young life—it would have broken my heart to see it cut short, with so much before it.''

Something caught at Ainn's heart, a quick fierce pain like a knife-thrust, that ripped through all her defenses. Her throat tightened, and she turned her heard away.

''Ainn?''

Ainn shuttered her thoughts. When she turned back to Thieras, her face was perfectly composed.

In the excitement of the journey, Thieras's eyes were as eager as they had been a summer ago. She had all the restlessness, the travel-hunger of her sea-born race. The broad shining waters of the estuary, the green willow-shaded valleys, the vast sweep of the downlands, all these for her were new and wondrous things. Almost, for those few days, she seemed to have put from her mind the desperateness of their purpose.

They made camp one night in a meadow; it was a place of power and good omen, at the confluence of three streams. The straight track that crossed it led to the old temple high on the downs, the site of Siod'h's circle. Nearby was a smaller temple, built by the tribe that lived in this valley, and sacred to the River-Lady.

The day had been hot; in the field by the three rivers the evening air was warm and soft as in the whitethorn month. There was no moon, but summer stars were flung across the sky as thick as daisies, casting a faint gleam of silver on the grass.

Thieras had thrown herself down on her cloak; with her hands folded behind her head, she began to search out, one by one, the constellations the priests had taught her.

After a while she said, in a small voice, ''All these will be here still, when we are gone.''

''Yes,'' Ainn said, hearing in those words an echo that went back to the first days of the world. ''I know. It is nights like this that are hardest to bear.''

Thieras gave her a sidelong look. ''Do you often think about it?'' she asked.

''About what, child?''

''About what will happen to us . . . when the sea comes.''

Ainn's eyes narrowed. ''I could say, maybe nothing will happen to us. And remind you of the purpose of this journey. Would you believe me?''

Thieras raised a skeptical eyebrow. ''You told me once, that we had no power, no magic, to hold back the sea.''

''I remember. I believed it at the time. Very likely it is true.''

''But even so . . .''

''Even so, I have been wrong before. As Ehlreth is wont to point out, our fates are written in sand, not stone. But no, lass, I will not offer you hope. I have watched you accept the certainty of your death, and accept it with good grace, because it was all we had to give you. To offer you false hope now, would be a crueler gift.'' She held Thieras's thin hand against her cheek. ''A chance to die with a semblance of honor, that is the best I can promise.''

''Dhan would say, that is promise enough for anyone,'' remarked Thieras. ''But still, no one wants to die.'' As she said that, her voice, which until now had been cool and oddly remote, had a sudden catch in it.

''Hardly anyone,'' amended Ainn. And Thieras gave her a wry smile, for she too had remembered that half-mad creature wandering on the beach, seeking in herbs and spells the release that death could not grant him.

''And yet,'' said Ainn, ''what is there in death, that is so frightening? It is in the last moments of life that the pain comes—and even so, men have suffered worse in battle, and lived.''

She stirred the fire, sending a shower of sparks flying up through the dark air. ''Like so,'' she said. ''Where are the flames when the fire goes out? Maybe that is how it will be for us. I have done with my life exactly what I chose to do. How many of us can say that, truly? Living longer, I will have lived no better." She looked down into Thieras's thoughtful eyes. "Girl, I know what you are thinking. When I was the age you are now, with all my choices yet to be made, and a dozen paths lying open before me—I would not have spoken then, as I do now. It is for you, for Siod'h, for Mara that I fight." She gave Thieras a rueful smile. "You see what has happened? I taught you to accept this thing. And now, when it comes to the point . . . Well," she finished. "Enough. Go to sleep now. We must be on our way again, before the sun comes up."

In the cold grey light before dawn they came in sight of Siod'h's temple: two great half-circles of stones, the one set within the other, with blue mist curling round their bases: somber black shapes against a colorless sky. Off to one side was a huddle of makeshift huts, and from among these a thin thread of smoke rose, but there was no other sign of life, nor was there any sound but the sad voice of the wind crying among the thorns.

Ainn shivered. There was something indescribably desolate about those broken circles, standing like ruins in that high, windswept, half-lit place.

As they came near, the first streaks of pink showed faintly in the east. Ainn chose her place: in the center of the avenue, between the two chalk banks, with the sunstone at her back.

The brightness in the east grew. Moments later the sun rose abruptly over the downs in a blaze of rose and violet light. Ainn stood still and quiet as the stones themselves, in that immense and waiting silence.

And then the call went forth—rushing out along the unseen lines of force that radiated from this still fixed center like the sun's beams, like spider's silk. Over the downs it went, over the wooded slopes and the hills and wolds yellow with the turning bracken, reaching as far as the northern isles, cross-

ing the fens and marshes, touching all the land lying green
and golden in that summer's dawn.

Everywhere in the lands of the west, everywhere the folk
of the Grey Isles had settled, where there was sorcerers'
blood, the call was heard, clear and compelling as a summons
into battle.

They came from the mists of the far isles, from the river
towns and the hill-camps, from the moors and marshes, from
the temples of grey stone and the deep places within the hills.
In their hundreds they came—men, women and youths,
priests, scholars and oracles, artists and healers, stone ma-
sons and warrior-kings. And the river-people came with
rafts, coracles, dugouts; waiting to ferry their kinfolk back to
the home-place, to the shores of the Grey Isles.

Ainn watched the gathering together of her people in the
temple grounds—the young men who had come for the sake
of honor, leaving wives and babes behind; the childless
women, and those whose children had grown—the stern set
of their mouths feigning a bravery their eyes belied. Their
homes and their hearts were elsewhere, in the gentle valleys
beyond the sea's reach, in the high heaths and the hill country. All the same, they had answered the call of the shared
blood, the ancient obligation.

After generations of intermarriage with the mainland folk,
there were as many blond heads as dark among them, with
eyes that were as often blue, or green, or brown, as winter-
grey. But each one of them, Ainn saw, was marked in some
fashion—with a high straight brow, a hawk nose, a look of
distance in the eyes, a long, sharp-cheekboned face. Each
one, in his or her own way, bore the clear sign of the
sorcerers' blood.

They stood waiting among the sycamore trees and the
standing stones. Their voices were hushed, their faces
somber. No strangers to magic, they were awed by the
ancient power and the sanctity of this place.

The day was overcast, the air dead calm, the sea smooth and pewter-colored. There was a tension in the air that pulled their nerves as taut as harpstrings.

Somewhere a dog was howling; the tide washed gently among the rocks; there was no other sound.

This should have been the time for the quiet ordering of thoughts, for spells and ceremonies, rituals of kinship and the slow in-gathering of power. So Ainn thought to herself, with bitter wisdom, when she realized the thing was at last beginning: for it is the way of the Old Gods always to catch us unprepared.

It was slight at first, a trembling and jolting like the many small shocks that had been felt of late. But this time the shuddering and heaving of the ground grew steadily more violent, until trees began to sway, and great waves and trenches rolled across the ground as though the earth had somehow been turned to water. There was a sound like the rushing of a great wind, though the air itself was still, and then an enormous grinding and rumbling that seemed to come from the ground beneath their feet. The noise was astounding, overwhelming, like the sound of huge rocks being wrenched asunder.

Eastward, behind the temple, a deep fissure opened in the earth, and the whole of the cliff-top on which they stood seemed to shift and tilt sideways, so that what had been level heathland sloped suddenly and precipitously toward the sea. Men and women screamed, and those nearest the cliff-edge threw themselves to their knees in terror, clutching roots and bushes as they scrambled up the steep incline.

The noise stopped as suddenly as it had begun; the sickening, lurching motion ceased. They stood dazed, speechless with shock, staring around them.

Though the temple itself seemed little damaged, the trees around it had been ripped out of the ground, exposing their great roots, and the fountain was smashed into a heap of rubble. Several of the tall stones had been uprooted and lay toppled on their sides; others leaned in unsteady balance. This perhaps more than anything unnerved the mainlanders, so much were their gifts of order and pattern bound up in the patterning of the stones.

All at once, instinctively, the people began to flow together, like drops of rainwater upon a glass; gathering within the circle of fallen stones, reaching out to one another with their hands, their minds, till what had been singular, discrete, became one creature, a many-headed, single-purposed being.

Ainn heard Thieras's small gasp of surprise; she too could feel that sense of merging, melding, that great surge of energy, like the rushing of water through joined streams. It was at once frightening and exhilarating, like a sudden leap from a high place.

Now the work could begin, the slow and complex interweaving of the threads of magic. Each one of them had been born with a gift of power. Of themselves, these were small gifts. Some could call the wind or still the waves, draw forth the rain from the clouds or charm the seed to flourish in barren ground. Not one among them had the strength or the skill to challenge the gods of the dark places, to bind their huge, inimical power. But now the magic came together, building, shaping. In Ainn's mind it was an arras they were making, of vast dimensions, woven with ancient runes in gold and silver thread: a thing as delicate as spider's silk, as strong and enduring as the forcelines of the earth.

Yet were there weak places in the fabric. Ainn could sense them, as one lifts a garment to the light and sees the thin places that will soon wear through. She saw, as through a mist, the face of the minstrel Eirech, and other faces that, like his, were self-absorbed, self-seeking: within the circle, yet no part of it. Their shapes, in her mind's eye, wavered and faded, like guttering candle-flames.

She wondered what had drawn them here—curiosity, malice, a blind instinct for self-preservation? Or perhaps in the end they had simply lacked the will to resist her summons.

She wove power into those weak places, as one darns silk. It left her drained, dizzy. The blood pounded in her ears. As though at a great distance she heard a voice calling out—uncertain at first, but gathering conviction.

"Look there!" the voice said. "Look there! By the Mother, we have won! We have beaten the sea back!"

Ainn looked, and suddenly she felt sick and faint. Like water in a tilted dish the ocean had withdrawn, had vastly and ominously retreated. What now lay exposed was a huge expanse of naked seabed, stretching beyond the limits of the lowest ebb-tide. As far as she could see, out past the entrance to the bay, there was glistening mud and weed-slimed rocks; fish squirming in the air among the rotting hulks of ancient ships.

Through the sheer power of her will Ainn gathered and held the loosening threads of magic. It was the hardest thing that she had ever done, like rejoining the slashed ends of arteries, knitting up the strands of severed nerves.

"Hold fast!" Her silent shout of command rang round the circle. "If the wall is to hold, it must hold now."

Through it all there was some small part of her mind that remained detached, so that she was able for an instant to look westward, seaward. There, rising at the mouth of the bay, she saw an enormous wall, a towering grey-green cliff of water. Massive and solid, spume-crested, it grew to colossal heights against the sky.

Ainn felt not so much fear as a vast astonishment. This, then, was the shadow in the stone, the dark vision: this monstrous upswelling, this rushing together of all the world's waters. It was more terrible, in the event, than anything she had imagined.

The others looked seaward then, and stared in horror: recognizing in that immense shape upon the horizon, the dreadful certainty of their fate.

The power of their joined minds faltered, weakened. Ainn felt a sudden sharp agony, as though some deep part of her flesh had been ripped away. The net of magic, the tapestry they had woven together, hung down in shreds like tattered silk.

. Ainn's arms tightened round Thieras's shoulders. "Be strong," she whispered. "The Lady is close by." The sky had vanished. Together they watched the grey immensity of waters gathering itself above them.

At the last there rose up in Ainn a fierce and sudden longing. In that final instant her mind leaped free, swift and wide in its searching, ranging outward, upward, with the sure power of a falcon's flight. Over immense distances of sea and forest it traveled, with a strength she had not imagined she possessed.

Alone on a northern hill, a young girl thought she heard her name spoken, felt a wistful touch like the wind's fingers upon her cheek. She turned, startled, found no one there. Her brow creased in momentary puzzlement; but, absorbed in the solid heft and balance of her first bronze blade, she quickly forgot that moment of strangeness.

Far to the south, a sailor dozing after a long watch stirred suddenly and sat up, feeling in his mind some faint wordless presence, like a gust of flower-scented wind. And understanding too well, he cried out in a bitter anguish of bereavement.

Ainn turned and hurled her voice like a challenge into the rising fury of the wind: defying to the end, in a voice like a battle trumpet, the huge indifferent face of death.

"They live!" she cried. There was rage in that shout, and a fierce joy, and triumph. "It is not ended yet. Dhan lives, and Mara. The Pattern remains!"

She felt Thieras's hand gripping hers, hard enough to crush the bone. She looked down into the hawkmaid's face. It was white to the lips, but the sea-grey eyes were steady.

There was a hissing like the voices of a million serpents; a vast and terrible roaring, like the sound of the wild surf but immeasurably louder. And then they were all a part of the thunder, and the darkness.

Although this is a work of fantasy, its roots spring from the fertile ground of Celtic pre-history and myth. Some of my sources were:

Atkinson, R.J.C. *Stonehenge*. Harmondsworth, Middlesex: Penguin, 1979 (rev.).

Garnier, C.M. "The Voyage of Maelduin," in *Legends of Ireland*. Cleveland, Ohio: World Publishing Co., 1968.

Higginson, Thomas Wentworth. *Tales of Atlantis and the Enchanted Isles*. North Hollywood: Newcastle, 1977 (reprint).

Hitching, Francis. *Earth Magic*. London: Cassell and Co., 1976.

Jacobs, Joseph, ed. *The Book of Wonder Voyages*. New York: G.P. Putnam's Sons.

Pepper, Elizabeth, and Wilcock, John. *A Guide to Magical and Mystical Sites in Europe and the British Isles*. New York: Harper & Row, 1977.

Severin, Tim. *The Brendan Voyage*. London: Hutchinson & Co., 1978.

Watkins, Alfred. *The Old Straight Track*. London: Sphere Books, 1974 (reprint).